# A CLASSIC CHRISTMAS

A COLLECTION OF TIMELESS

STORIES AND POEMS

THOMAS NELSON
*Since 1798*

**Library of Congress Cataloging-in-Publication Data**

Title: A classic Christmas : a collection of timeless stories and poems.
Description: [Nashville, Tenn.] : Thomas Nelson, [2019]
Identifiers: LCCN 2019015552| ISBN 9780785232223 (hardcover) | ISBN 9780785232278 (e-book)
Subjects: LCSH: Christmas--Literary collections. | Christmas stories. | Christmas poetry.
Classification: LCC PN6071.C6 C64 2019 | DDC 808.8/0334--dc23 LC record available at https://lccn.loc.gov/2019015552

*Printed in the United States of America*
19 20 21 22 23 LSC 5 4 3 2 1

# CONTENTS

## STORIES AND SKETCHES

# CONTENTS

## POEMS

IV

# STORIES AND SKETCHES

# CHARLES DICKENS

1812-1870

# A CHRISTMAS CAROL

# PREFACE

I have endeavoured in this Ghostly little book, to raise the Ghost of an Idea, which shall not put my readers out of humour with themselves, with each other, with the season, or with me. May it haunt their houses pleasantly, and no one wish to lay it.

> Their faithful Friend
> and Servant,
> C. D.

## Stave One

# MARLEY'S GHOST

Marley was dead: to begin with. There is no doubt whatever about that. The register of his burial was signed by the clergyman, the clerk, the undertaker, and the chief mourner. Scrooge signed it: and Scrooge's name was good upon 'Change, for anything he chose to put his hand to. Old Marley was as dead as a door-nail.

Mind! I don't mean to say that I know, of my own knowledge, what there is particularly dead about a door-nail. I might have been inclined, myself, to regard a coffin-nail as the deadest piece of ironmongery in the trade. But the wisdom of our ancestors is in the simile; and my unhallowed hands shall not disturb it, or the Country's done for. You will therefore permit me to repeat, emphatically, that Marley was as dead as a door-nail.

Scrooge knew he was dead? Of course he did. How could it be otherwise? Scrooge and he were partners for I don't know how many years. Scrooge was his sole executor, his sole administrator, his sole assign, his sole residuary legatee, his sole friend, and sole mourner. And even Scrooge was not so dreadfully cut up by the sad event, but that he was an excellent man of business on the very day of the funeral, and solemnised it with an undoubted bargain.

The mention of Marley's funeral brings me back to the point I started from. There is no doubt that Marley was dead. This must be distinctly understood, or nothing wonderful can come of the story I am going to relate. If we were not perfectly convinced that Hamlet's Father died before the play began, there would be nothing more remarkable in his taking a stroll at night, in an easterly wind, upon his own ramparts, than there would be in any other middle-aged gentleman rashly turning out after dark in a breezy spot—say Saint Paul's Churchyard for instance—literally to astonish his son's weak mind.

Scrooge never painted out Old Marley's name. There it stood, years afterwards, above the warehouse door: Scrooge and Marley. The firm was known as Scrooge and Marley. Sometimes people new to the business called Scrooge Scrooge, and sometimes Marley, but he answered to both names. It was all the same to him.

Oh! But he was a tight-fisted hand at the grindstone, Scrooge! a squeezing, wrenching, grasping, scraping, clutching, covetous, old sinner! Hard and sharp as flint, from which no steel had ever struck out generous fire; secret, and self-contained, and solitary as an oyster. The cold within him froze his old features, nipped his pointed nose, shrivelled his cheek, stiffened his gait; made his eyes red, his thin lips blue; and spoke out shrewdly in his grating voice. A frosty rime was on his head, and on his eyebrows, and his wiry chin. He carried his own low temperature always about with him; he iced his office in the dog-days; and didn't thaw it one degree at Christmas.

External heat and cold had little influence on Scrooge. No warmth could warm, no wintry weather chill him. No wind that blew was bitterer than he, no falling snow was more intent upon its purpose, no pelting rain less open to entreaty. Foul weather didn't know where to have him. The heaviest rain, and snow, and hail, and sleet, could boast of the advantage over him in only one respect. They often "came down" handsomely, and Scrooge never did.

Nobody ever stopped him in the street to say, with gladsome looks, "My dear Scrooge, how are you? When will you come to see me?" No beggars implored him to bestow a trifle, no children asked him what it was o'clock, no man or woman ever once in all his life inquired the way to such and such a place, of Scrooge. Even the blind men's dogs appeared to know him; and when they saw him coming on, would tug their owners into doorways and up courts; and then would wag their tails as though they said, "No eye at all is better than an evil eye, dark master!"

But what did Scrooge care! It was the very thing he liked. To edge his way along the crowded paths of life, warning all human sympathy to keep its distance, was what the knowing ones call "nuts" to Scrooge.

Once upon a time—of all the good days in the year, on Christmas Eve—old Scrooge sat busy in his counting-house. It was cold, bleak, biting weather: foggy withal: and he could hear the people in the court outside, go wheezing up and down, beating their hands upon their breasts, and stamping their feet upon the pavement stones to warm them. The city clocks had only just gone three, but it was quite dark already—it had not been light all day—and candles were flaring in the windows of the neighbouring offices, like ruddy smears upon the palpable brown air. The fog came pouring in at every chink and key-hole, and was so dense without, that although the court was of the narrowest, the houses opposite were mere phantoms. To see the dingy cloud come drooping down, obscuring everything, one might have thought that Nature lived hard by, and was brewing on a large scale.

The door of Scrooge's counting-house was open that he might keep his eye upon his clerk, who in a dismal little cell beyond, a sort of tank, was copying letters. Scrooge had a very small fire, but the clerk's fire was so very much smaller that it looked like one coal. But he couldn't replenish it, for Scrooge kept the coal-box in his own room; and so surely as the clerk came in with the shovel, the master predicted that it would be necessary for them to part. Wherefore the clerk put on his white comforter, and tried to warm himself at the candle; in which effort, not being a man of a strong imagination, he failed.

"A merry Christmas, uncle! God save you!" cried a cheerful voice. It was the voice of Scrooge's nephew, who came upon him so quickly that this was the first intimation he had of his approach.

"Bah!" said Scrooge, "Humbug!"

He had so heated himself with rapid walking in the fog and frost, this nephew of Scrooge's, that he was all in a glow; his face was ruddy and handsome; his eyes sparkled, and his breath smoked again.

"Christmas a humbug, uncle!" said Scrooge's nephew. "You don't mean that, I am sure?"

"I do," said Scrooge. "Merry Christmas! What right have you to be merry? What reason have you to be merry? You're poor enough."

"Come, then," returned the nephew gaily. "What right have you to be dismal? What reason have you to be morose? You're rich enough."

Scrooge having no better answer ready on the

spur of the moment, said, "Bah!" again; and followed it up with "Humbug."

"Don't be cross, uncle!" said the nephew.

"What else can I be," returned the uncle, "when I live in such a world of fools as this? Merry Christmas! Out upon merry Christmas! What's Christmas time to you but a time for paying bills without money; a time for finding yourself a year older, but not an hour richer; a time for balancing your books and having every item in 'em through a round dozen of months presented dead against you? If I could work my will," said Scrooge indignantly, "every idiot who goes about with 'Merry Christmas' on his lips, should be boiled with his own pudding, and buried with a stake of holly through his heart. He should!"

"Uncle!" pleaded the nephew.

"Nephew!" returned the uncle sternly, "keep Christmas in your own way, and let me keep it in mine."

"Keep it!" repeated Scrooge's nephew. "But you don't keep it."

"Let me leave it alone, then," said Scrooge. "Much good may it do you! Much good it has ever done you!"

"There are many things from which I might have derived good, by which I have not profited, I dare say," returned the nephew. "Christmas among the rest. But I am sure I have always thought of Christmas time, when it has come round—apart from the veneration due to its sacred name and origin, if anything belonging to it can be apart from that—as a good time; a kind, forgiving, charitable, pleasant time; the only time I know of, in the long calendar of the year, when men and women seem by one consent to open their shut-up hearts freely, and to think of people below them as if they really were fellow-passengers to the grave, and not another race of creatures bound on other journeys. And therefore, uncle, though it has never put a scrap of gold or silver in my pocket, I believe that it *has* done me good, and *will* do me good; and I say, God bless it!"

The clerk in the Tank involuntarily applauded. Becoming immediately sensible of the impropriety, he poked the fire, and extinguished the last frail spark for ever.

"Let me hear another sound from *you*," said Scrooge, "and you'll keep your Christmas by losing your situation! You're quite a powerful speaker, sir," he added, turning to his nephew. "I wonder you don't go into Parliament."

"Don't be angry, uncle. Come! Dine with us to-morrow."

Scrooge said that he would see him—yes, indeed he did. He went the whole length of the expression, and said that he would see him in that extremity first.

"But why?" cried Scrooge's nephew. "Why?"

"Why did you get married?" said Scrooge.

"Because I fell in love."

"Because you fell in love!" growled Scrooge, as if that were the only one thing in the world more ridiculous than a merry Christmas. "Good afternoon!"

"Nay, uncle, but you never came to see me before that happened. Why give it as a reason for not coming now?"

"Good afternoon," said Scrooge.

"I want nothing from you; I ask nothing of you; why cannot we be friends?"

"Good afternoon," said Scrooge.

"I am sorry, with all my heart, to find you so resolute. We have never had any quarrel, to which I have been a party. But I have made the trial in homage to Christmas, and I'll keep my Christmas humour to the last. So a Merry Christmas, uncle!"

"Good afternoon!" said Scrooge.

"And a Happy New Year!"

"Good afternoon!" said Scrooge.

His nephew left the room without an angry word, notwithstanding. He stopped at the outer door to bestow the greetings of the season on the clerk, who, cold as he was, was warmer than Scrooge; for he returned them cordially.

"There's another fellow," muttered Scrooge, who overheard him: "my clerk, with fifteen shillings a week, and a wife and family, talking about a merry Christmas. I'll retire to Bedlam."

This lunatic, in letting Scrooge's nephew out, had let two other people in. They were portly gentlemen, pleasant to behold, and now stood, with their hats off, in Scrooge's office. They had books and papers in their hands, and bowed to him.

"Scrooge and Marley's, I believe," said one of the gentlemen, referring to his list. "Have I the pleasure of addressing Mr. Scrooge, or Mr. Marley?"

"Mr. Marley has been dead these seven years," Scrooge replied. "He died seven years ago, this very night."

"We have no doubt his liberality is well represented by his surviving partner," said the gentleman, presenting his credentials.

It certainly was; for they had been two kindred spirits. At the ominous word "liberality," Scrooge frowned, and shook his head, and handed the credentials back.

"At this festive season of the year, Mr. Scrooge," said the gentleman, taking up a pen, "it is more than usually desirable that we should make some slight provision for the Poor and destitute, who suffer greatly at the present time. Many thousands are in want of common necessaries; hundreds of thousands are in want of common comforts, sir."

"Are there no prisons?" asked Scrooge.

"Plenty of prisons," said the gentleman, laying down the pen again.

"And the Union workhouses?" demanded Scrooge. "Are they still in operation?"

"They are. Still," returned the gentleman, "I wish I could say they were not."

"The Treadmill and the Poor Law are in full vigour, then?" said Scrooge.

"Both very busy, sir."

"Oh! I was afraid, from what you said at first, that something had occurred to stop them in their useful course," said Scrooge. "I'm very glad to hear it."

"Under the impression that they scarcely furnish Christian cheer of mind or body to the multitude," returned the gentleman, "a few of us are endeavouring to raise a fund to buy the Poor some meat and drink, and means of warmth. We choose this time, because it is a time, of all others, when Want is keenly felt, and Abundance rejoices. What shall I put you down for?"

"Nothing!" Scrooge replied.

"You wish to be anonymous?"

"I wish to be left alone," said Scrooge. "Since you ask me what I wish, gentlemen, that is my answer. I don't make merry myself at Christmas and I can't afford to make idle people merry. I help to support the establishments I have mentioned—they cost enough; and those who are badly off must go there."

"Many can't go there; and many would rather die."

"If they would rather die," said Scrooge, "they had better do it, and decrease the surplus population. Besides—excuse me—I don't know that."

"But you might know it," observed the gentleman.

"It's not my business," Scrooge returned. "It's enough for a man to understand his own business, and not to interfere with other people's. Mine occupies me constantly. Good afternoon, gentlemen!"

Seeing clearly that it would be useless to pursue their point, the gentlemen withdrew. Scrooge resumed his labours with an improved opinion of himself, and in a more facetious temper than was usual with him.

Meanwhile the fog and darkness thickened so, that people ran about with flaring links, proffering their services to go before horses in carriages, and conduct them on their way. The ancient tower of a church, whose gruff old bell was always peeping slily down at Scrooge out of a Gothic window in the wall, became invisible, and struck the hours and quarters in the clouds, with tremulous vibrations afterwards as if its teeth were chattering in its frozen head up there. The cold became intense. In the main street, at the corner of the court, some labourers were repairing the gas-pipes, and had lighted a great fire in a brazier, round which a party of ragged men and boys were gathered: warming their hands and winking their eyes before the blaze in rapture. The water-plug being left in solitude, its overflowings sullenly congealed, and turned to misanthropic ice. The brightness of the shops where holly sprigs and berries crackled in the lamp heat of the windows, made pale faces ruddy as they passed. Poulterers' and grocers' trades became a splendid joke: a glorious pageant, with which it was next to impossible to believe that such dull principles as bargain and sale had anything to do. The Lord Mayor, in the strong-hold of the mighty Mansion House, gave orders to his fifty cooks and butlers to keep Christmas as a Lord Mayor's household should; and even the little tailor, whom he had fined five shillings on the previous Monday for being drunk and bloodthirsty in the streets, stirred up to-morrow's pudding in his garret, while his lean wife and the baby sallied out to buy the beef.

Foggier yet, and colder. Piercing, searching, biting cold. If the good Saint Dunstan had but nipped the Evil Spirit's nose with a touch of such weather as that, instead of using his familiar weapons, then indeed he would have roared to lusty purpose. The owner of one scant young nose, gnawed and mumbled by the hungry cold as bones are gnawed by dogs, stooped down at Scrooge's keyhole to regale him with a Christmas carol: but at the first sound of

"God bless you, merry gentleman!
May nothing you dismay!"

Scrooge seized the ruler with such energy of action, that the singer fled in terror, leaving the key-hole to the fog and even more congenial frost.

At length the hour of shutting up the counting-house arrived. With an ill-will Scrooge dismounted from his stool, and tacitly admitted the fact to the expectant clerk in the Tank, who instantly snuffed his candle out, and put on his hat.

"You'll want all day to-morrow, I suppose?" said Scrooge.

"If quite convenient, sir."

"It's not convenient," said Scrooge, "and it's not fair. If I was to stop half-a-crown for it, you'd think yourself ill-used, I'll be bound?"

The clerk smiled faintly.

"And yet," said Scrooge, "you don't think *me* ill-used, when I pay a day's wages for no work."

The clerk observed that it was only once a year.

"A poor excuse for picking a man's pocket every twenty-fifth of December!" said Scrooge, buttoning his great-coat to the chin. "But I suppose you must have the whole day. Be here all the earlier next morning."

The clerk promised that he would; and Scrooge walked out with a growl. The office was closed in a twinkling, and the clerk, with the long ends of his white comforter dangling below his waist (for he boasted no great-coat), went down a slide on Cornhill, at the end of a lane of boys, twenty times, in honour of its being Christmas Eve, and then ran home to Camden Town as hard as he could pelt, to play at blind-man's buff.

Scrooge took his melancholy dinner in his usual

melancholy tavern; and having read all the news-papers, and beguiled the rest of the evening with his banker's-book, went home to bed. He lived in chambers which had once belonged to his deceased partner. They were a gloomy suite of rooms, in a low-ering pile of building up a yard, where it had so little business to be, that one could scarcely help fancying it must have run there when it was a young house, playing at hide-and-seek with other houses, and for-gotten the way out again. It was old enough now, and dreary enough, for nobody lived in it but Scrooge, the other rooms being all let out as offices. The yard was so dark that even Scrooge, who knew its every stone, was fain to grope with his hands. The fog and frost so hung about the black old gateway of the house, that it seemed as if the Genius of the Weather sat in mournful meditation on the threshold.

Now, it is a fact, that there was nothing at all particular about the knocker on the door, except that it was very large. It is also a fact, that Scrooge had seen it, night and morning, during his whole residence in that place; also that Scrooge had as little of what is called fancy about him as any man in the city of London, even including—which is a bold word—the corporation, aldermen, and livery. Let it also be borne in mind that Scrooge had not bestowed one thought on Marley, since his last mention of his seven years' dead partner that afternoon. And then let any man explain to me, if he can, how it happened that Scrooge, having his key in the lock of the door, saw in the knocker, without its undergoing any intermediate process of change—not a knocker, but Marley's face.

Marley's face. It was not in impenetrable shadow as the other objects in the yard were, but had a dismal light about it, like a bad lobster in a dark cellar. It was not angry or ferocious, but looked at Scrooge as Marley used to look: with ghostly spectacles turned up on its ghostly forehead. The hair was curiously stirred, as if by breath or hot air; and, though the eyes were wide open, they were perfectly motionless. That, and its livid colour, made it horrible; but its horror seemed to be in spite of the face and beyond its control, rather than a part of its own expression.

As Scrooge looked fixedly at this phenomenon, it was a knocker again.

To say that he was not startled, or that his blood was not conscious of a terrible sensation to which it had been a stranger from infancy, would be untrue. But he put his hand upon the key he had relinquished, turned it sturdily, walked in, and lighted his candle.

He *did* pause, with a moment's irresolution, before he shut the door; and he *did* look cautiously behind it first, as if he half expected to be terrified with the sight of Marley's pigtail sticking out into the hall. But there was nothing on the back of the door, except the screws and nuts that held the knocker on, so he said, "Pooh, pooh!" and closed it with a bang.

The sound resounded through the house like thunder. Every room above, and every cask in the wine-merchant's cellars below, appeared to have a separate peal of echoes of its own. Scrooge was not a man to be frightened by echoes. He fastened the door, and walked across the hall, and up the stairs; slowly too: trimming his candle as he went.

You may talk vaguely about driving a coach-and-six up a good old flight of stairs, or through a bad young Act of Parliament; but I mean to say you might have got a hearse up that staircase, and taken it broadwise, with the splinter-bar towards the wall and the door towards the balustrades: and done it easy. There was plenty of width for that, and room to spare; which is perhaps the reason why Scrooge thought he saw a locomotive hearse going on before him in the gloom. Half-a-dozen gas-lamps out of the street wouldn't have lighted the entry too well, so you may suppose that it was pretty dark with Scrooge's dip.

Up Scrooge went, not caring a button for that. Darkness is cheap, and Scrooge liked it. But before he shut his heavy door, he walked through his rooms to see that all was right. He had just enough recollection of the face to desire to do that.

Sitting-room, bedroom, lumber-room. All as they should be. Nobody under the table, nobody under the sofa; a small fire in the grate; spoon and basin ready; and the little saucepan of gruel (Scrooge had a cold in his head) upon the hob. Nobody under the bed; nobody in the closet; nobody in his dressing-gown, which was hanging up in a suspicious attitude against the wall. Lumber-room as usual. Old fire-guard, old shoes, two fish-baskets, washing-stand on three legs, and a poker.

Quite satisfied, he closed his door, and locked himself in; double-locked himself in, which was not his custom. Thus secured against surprise, he took off his cravat; put on his dressing-gown and slippers, and his nightcap; and sat down before the fire to take his gruel.

It was a very low fire indeed; nothing on such a bitter night. He was obliged to sit close to it, and brood over it, before he could extract the least sensation of warmth from such a handful of fuel. The fireplace was an old one, built by some Dutch merchant long ago, and paved all round with quaint Dutch tiles, designed to illustrate the Scriptures. There were Cains and Abels, Pharaoh's daughters; Queens of Sheba, Angelic messengers descending through the air on clouds like feather-beds, Abrahams, Belshazzars, Apostles putting off to sea in butter-boats, hundreds of figures to attract his thoughts; and yet that face of Marley, seven years dead, came like the ancient Prophet's rod, and swallowed up the whole. If each smooth tile had been a blank at first, with power to shape some picture on its surface from the disjointed fragments of his thoughts, there would have been a copy of old Marley's head on every one.

"Humbug!" said Scrooge; and walked across the room.

After several turns, he sat down again. As he threw his head back in the chair, his glance happened to rest upon a bell, a disused bell, that hung in the room, and communicated for some purpose now forgotten with a chamber in the highest story of the building. It was with great astonishment, and with a strange, inexplicable dread, that as he looked, he saw this bell begin to swing. It swung so softly in the outset that it scarcely made a sound; but soon it rang out loudly, and so did every bell in the house.

This might have lasted half a minute, or a minute, but it seemed an hour. The bells ceased as they had begun, together. They were succeeded by a clanking noise, deep down below; as if some person were dragging a heavy chain over the casks in the wine-merchant's cellar. Scrooge then remembered to have heard that ghosts in haunted houses were described as dragging chains.

The cellar-door flew open with a booming sound,

and then he heard the noise much louder, on the floors below; then coming up the stairs; then coming straight towards his door.

"It's humbug still!" said Scrooge. "I won't believe it."

His colour changed though, when, without a pause, it came on through the heavy door, and passed into the room before his eyes. Upon its coming in, the dying flame leaped up, as though it cried, "I know him; Marley's Ghost!" and fell again.

The same face: the very same. Marley in his pig-tail, usual waistcoat, tights and boots; the tassels on the latter bristling, like his pigtail, and his coat-skirts, and the hair upon his head. The chain he drew was clasped about his middle. It was long, and wound about him like a tail; and it was made (for Scrooge observed it closely) of cash-boxes, keys, padlocks, ledgers, deeds, and heavy purses wrought in steel. His body was transparent; so that Scrooge, observing him, and looking through his waistcoat, could see the two buttons on his coat behind.

Scrooge had often heard it said that Marley had no bowels, but he had never believed it until now.

No, nor did he believe it even now. Though he looked the phantom through and through, and saw it standing before him; though he felt the chilling influence of its death-cold eyes; and marked the very texture of the folded kerchief bound about its head and chin, which wrapper he had not observed before; he was still incredulous, and fought against his senses.

"How now!" said Scrooge, caustic and cold as ever. "What do you want with me?"

"Much!"—Marley's voice, no doubt about it.

"Who are you?"

"Ask me who I *was*."

"Who *were* you then?" said Scrooge, raising his voice. "You're particular, for a shade." He was going to say "*to* a shade," but substituted this, as more appropriate.

"In life I was your partner, Jacob Marley."

"Can you—can you sit down?" asked Scrooge, looking doubtfully at him.

"I can."

"Do it, then."

Scrooge asked the question, because he didn't know whether a ghost so transparent might find himself in a condition to take a chair; and felt that in the event of its being impossible, it might involve the necessity of an embarrassing explanation. But the ghost sat down on the opposite side of the fireplace, as if he were quite used to it.

"You don't believe in me," observed the Ghost.

"I don't," said Scrooge.

"What evidence would you have of my reality beyond that of your senses?"

"I don't know," said Scrooge.

"Why do you doubt your senses?"

"Because," said Scrooge, "a little thing affects them. A slight disorder of the stomach makes them cheats. You may be an undigested bit of beef, a blot of mustard, a crumb of cheese, a fragment of an underdone potato. There's more of gravy than of grave about you, whatever you are!"

Scrooge was not much in the habit of cracking jokes, nor did he feel, in his heart, by any means waggish then. The truth is, that he tried to be smart, as a means of distracting his own attention, and keeping down his terror; for the spectre's voice disturbed the very marrow in his bones.

To sit, staring at those fixed glazed eyes, in silence for a moment, would play, Scrooge felt, the very deuce with him. There was something very awful, too, in the spectre's being provided with an infernal atmosphere of its own. Scrooge could not feel it himself, but this was clearly the case; for though the Ghost sat perfectly motionless, its hair, and skirts, and tassels, were still agitated as by the hot vapour from an oven.

"You see this toothpick?" said Scrooge, returning quickly to the charge, for the reason just assigned; and wishing, though it were only for a second, to divert the vision's stony gaze from himself.

"I do," replied the Ghost.

"You are not looking at it," said Scrooge.

"But I see it," said the Ghost, "notwithstanding."

"Well!" returned Scrooge, "I have but to swallow this, and be for the rest of my days persecuted by a legion of goblins, all of my own creation. Humbug, I tell you! humbug!"

At this the spirit raised a frightful cry, and shook its chain with such a dismal and appalling noise, that Scrooge held on tight to his chair, to save himself from falling in a swoon. But how much greater was his horror, when the phantom taking off the bandage round its head, as if it were too warm to wear indoors, its lower jaw dropped down upon its breast!

Scrooge fell upon his knees, and clasped his hands before his face.

"Mercy!" he said. "Dreadful apparition, why do you trouble me?"

"Man of the worldly mind!" replied the Ghost, "do you believe in me or not?"

"I do," said Scrooge. "I must. But why do spirits walk the earth, and why do they come to me?"

"It is required of every man," the Ghost returned, "that the spirit within him should walk abroad among his fellowmen, and travel far and wide; and if that spirit goes not forth in life, it is condemned to do so after death. It is doomed to wander through the world—oh, woe is me!—and witness what it cannot share, but might have shared on earth, and turned to happiness!"

Again the spectre raised a cry, and shook its chain and wrung its shadowy hands.

"You are fettered," said Scrooge, trembling. "Tell me why?"

"I wear the chain I forged in life," replied the Ghost. "I made it link by link, and yard by yard; I girded it on of my own free will, and of my own free will I wore it. Is its pattern strange to *you*?"

Scrooge trembled more and more.

"Or would you know," pursued the Ghost, "the weight and length of the strong coil you bear yourself? It was full as heavy and as long as this, seven Christmas Eves ago. You have laboured on it, since. It is a ponderous chain!"

Scrooge glanced about him on the floor, in the expectation of finding himself surrounded by some fifty or sixty fathoms of iron cable: but he could see nothing.

"Jacob," he said, imploringly. "Old Jacob Marley, tell me more. Speak comfort to me, Jacob!"

"I have none to give," the Ghost replied. "It comes from other regions, Ebenezer Scrooge, and is conveyed by other ministers, to other kinds of men. Nor can I tell you what I would. A very little more is all permitted to me. I cannot rest, I cannot stay,

I cannot linger anywhere. My spirit never walked beyond our counting-house—mark me!—in life my spirit never roved beyond the narrow limits of our money-changing hole; and weary journeys lie before me!"

It was a habit with Scrooge, whenever he became thoughtful, to put his hands in his breeches pockets. Pondering on what the Ghost had said, he did so now, but without lifting up his eyes, or getting off his knees.

"You must have been very slow about it, Jacob," Scrooge observed, in a business-like manner, though with humility and deference.

"Slow!" the Ghost repeated.

"Seven years dead," mused Scrooge. "And travelling all the time!"

"The whole time," said the Ghost. "No rest, no peace. Incessant torture of remorse."

"You travel fast?" said Scrooge.

"On the wings of the wind," replied the Ghost.

"You might have got over a great quantity of ground in seven years," said Scrooge.

The Ghost, on hearing this, set up another cry,

and clanked its chain so hideously in the dead silence of the night, that the Ward would have been justified in indicting it for a nuisance.

"Oh! captive, bound, and double-ironed," cried the phantom, "not to know, that ages of incessant labour by immortal creatures, for this earth must pass into eternity before the good of which it is susceptible is all developed. Not to know that any Christian spirit working kindly in its little sphere, whatever it may be, will find its mortal life too short for its vast means of usefulness. Not to know that no space of regret can make amends for one life's opportunity misused! Yet such was I! Oh! such was I!"

"But you were always a good man of business, Jacob," faltered Scrooge, who now began to apply this to himself.

"Business!" cried the Ghost, wringing its hands again. "Mankind was my business. The common welfare was my business; charity, mercy, forbearance, and benevolence, were, all, my business. The dealings of my trade were but a drop of water in the comprehensive ocean of my business!"

It held up its chain at arm's length, as if that were

the cause of all its unavailing grief, and flung it heavily upon the ground again.

"At this time of the rolling year," the spectre said, "I suffer most. Why did I walk through crowds of fellow-beings with my eyes turned down, and never raise them to that blessed Star which led the Wise Men to a poor abode! Were there no poor homes to which its light would have conducted *me*!"

Scrooge was very much dismayed to hear the spectre going on at this rate, and began to quake exceedingly.

"Hear me!" cried the Ghost. "My time is nearly gone."

"I will," said Scrooge. "But don't be hard upon me! Don't be flowery, Jacob! Pray!"

"How it is that I appear before you in a shape that you can see, I may not tell. I have sat invisible beside you many and many a day."

It was not an agreeable idea. Scrooge shivered, and wiped the perspiration from his brow.

"That is no light part of my penance," pursued the Ghost. "I am here to-night to warn you, that you have yet a chance and hope of escaping my fate. A chance and hope of my procuring, Ebenezer."

"You were always a good friend to me," said Scrooge. "Thank'ee!"

"You will be haunted," resumed the Ghost, "by Three Spirits."

Scrooge's countenance fell almost as low as the Ghost's had done.

"Is that the chance and hope you mentioned, Jacob?" he demanded, in a faltering voice.

"It is."

"I—I think I'd rather not," said Scrooge.

"Without their visits," said the Ghost, "you cannot hope to shun the path I tread. Expect the first to-morrow, when the bell tolls One."

"Couldn't I take 'em all at once, and have it over, Jacob?" hinted Scrooge.

"Expect the second on the next night at the same hour. The third upon the next night when the last stroke of Twelve has ceased to vibrate. Look to see me no more; and look that, for your own sake, you remember what has passed between us!"

When it had said these words, the spectre took its wrapper from the table, and bound it round its head, as before. Scrooge knew this, by the smart sound its teeth made, when the jaws were brought together by the bandage. He ventured to raise his eyes again, and found his supernatural visitor confronting him in an erect attitude, with its chain wound over and about its arm.

The apparition walked backward from him; and at every step it took, the window raised itself a little, so that when the spectre reached it, it was wide open.

It beckoned Scrooge to approach, which he did. When they were within two paces of each other, Marley's Ghost held up its hand, warning him to come no nearer. Scrooge stopped.

Not so much in obedience, as in surprise and fear: for on the raising of the hand, he became sensible of confused noises in the air; incoherent sounds of lamentation and regret; wailings inexpressibly sorrowful and self-accusatory. The spectre, after listening for a moment, joined in the mournful dirge; and floated out upon the bleak, dark night.

Scrooge followed to the window: desperate in his curiosity. He looked out.

The air was filled with phantoms, wandering

hither and thither in restless haste, and moaning as they went. Every one of them wore chains like Marley's Ghost; some few (they might be guilty governments) were linked together; none were free. Many had been personally known to Scrooge in their lives. He had been quite familiar with one old ghost, in a white waistcoat, with a monstrous iron safe attached to its ankle, who cried piteously at being unable to assist a wretched woman with an infant, whom it saw below, upon a door-step. The misery with them all was, clearly, that they sought to interfere, for good, in human matters, and had lost the power for ever.

Whether these creatures faded into mist, or mist enshrouded them, he could not tell. But they and their spirit voices faded together; and the night became as it had been when he walked home.

Scrooge closed the window, and examined the door by which the Ghost had entered. It was double-locked, as he had locked it with his own hands, and the bolts were undisturbed. He tried to say, "Humbug!" but stopped at the first syllable. And being, from the emotion he had undergone, or the fatigues of the day, or his glimpse of the Invisible World, or the dull conversation of the Ghost, or the lateness of the hour, much in need of repose; went straight to bed, without undressing, and fell asleep upon the instant.

## Stave Two

# THE FIRST OF THE THREE SPIRITS

When Scrooge awoke, it was so dark, that looking out of bed, he could scarcely distinguish the transparent window from the opaque walls of his chamber. He was endeavouring to pierce the darkness with his ferret eyes, when the chimes of a neighbouring church struck the four quarters. So he listened for the hour.

To his great astonishment the heavy bell went on from six to seven, and from seven to eight, and regularly up to twelve; then stopped. Twelve! It was past two when he went to bed. The clock was wrong. An icicle must have got into the works. Twelve!

He touched the spring of his repeater, to correct

this most preposterous clock. Its rapid little pulse beat twelve: and stopped.

"Why, it isn't possible," said Scrooge, "that I can have slept through a whole day and far into another night. It isn't possible that anything has happened to the sun, and this is twelve at noon!"

The idea being an alarming one, he scrambled out of bed, and groped his way to the window. He was obliged to rub the frost off with the sleeve of his dressing-gown before he could see anything; and could see very little then. All he could make out was, that it was still very foggy and extremely cold, and that there was no noise of people running to and fro, and making a great stir, as there unquestionably would have been if night had beaten off bright day, and taken possession of the world. This was a great relief, because "three days after sight of this First of Exchange pay to Mr. Ebenezer Scrooge or his order," and so forth, would have become a mere United States' security if there were no days to count by.

Scrooge went to bed again, and thought, and thought, and thought it over and over and over, and could make nothing of it. The more he thought, the more perplexed he was; and the more he endeavoured not to think, the more he thought.

Marley's Ghost bothered him exceedingly. Every time he resolved within himself, after mature inquiry, that it was all a dream, his mind flew back again, like a strong spring released, to its first position, and presented the same problem to be worked all through, "Was it a dream or not?"

Scrooge lay in this state until the chime had gone three-quarters more, when he remembered, on a sudden, that the Ghost had warned him of a visitation when the bell tolled one. He resolved to lie awake until the hour was passed; and, considering that he could no more go to sleep than go to Heaven, this was perhaps the wisest resolution in his power.

The quarter was so long, that he was more than once convinced he must have sunk into a doze unconsciously, and missed the clock. At length it broke upon his listening ear.

"Ding, dong!"

"A quarter past," said Scrooge, counting.

"Ding, dong!"

"Half-past!" said Scrooge.

"Ding, dong!"

"A quarter to it," said Scrooge.

"Ding, dong!"

"The hour itself," said Scrooge, triumphantly, "and nothing else!"

He spoke before the hour bell sounded, which it now did with a deep, dull, hollow, melancholy ONE. Light flashed up in the room upon the instant, and the curtains of his bed were drawn.

The curtains of his bed were drawn aside, I tell you, by a hand. Not the curtains at his feet, nor the curtains at his back, but those to which his face was addressed. The curtains of his bed were drawn aside; and Scrooge, starting up into a half-recumbent attitude, found himself face to face with the unearthly visitor who drew them: as close to it as I am now to you, and I am standing in the spirit at your elbow.

It was a strange figure—like a child: yet not so like a child as like an old man, viewed through some supernatural medium, which gave him the appearance of having receded from the view, and being diminished to a child's proportions. Its hair, which hung about its neck and down its back, was white as if with age; and yet the face had not a wrinkle in it, and the tenderest bloom was on the skin. The arms were very long and muscular; the hands the same, as if its hold were of uncommon strength. Its legs and feet, most delicately formed, were, like those upper members, bare. It wore a tunic of the purest white; and round its waist was bound a lustrous belt, the sheen of which was beautiful. It held a branch of fresh green holly in its hand; and, in singular contradiction of that wintry emblem, had its dress trimmed with summer flowers. But the strangest thing about it was, that from the crown of its head there sprung a bright clear jet of light, by which all this was visible; and which was doubtless the occasion of its using, in its duller moments, a great extinguisher for a cap, which it now held under its arm.

Even this, though, when Scrooge looked at it with increasing steadiness, was *not* its strangest quality. For as its belt sparkled and glittered now in one part and now in another, and what was light one instant, at another time was dark, so the figure itself fluctuated in its distinctness: being now a thing with one arm, now with one leg, now with twenty legs, now a pair of legs without a head, now a head without a body: of which dissolving parts, no outline would be visible in the dense gloom wherein they melted away. And in the very wonder of this, it would be itself again; distinct and clear as ever.

"Are you the Spirit, sir, whose coming was foretold to me?" asked Scrooge.

"I am!"

The voice was soft and gentle. Singularly low, as if instead of being so close beside him, it were at a distance.

"Who, and what are you?" Scrooge demanded.

"I am the Ghost of Christmas Past."

"Long Past?" inquired Scrooge: observant of its dwarfish stature.

"No. Your past."

Perhaps, Scrooge could not have told anybody why, if anybody could have asked him; but he had a special desire to see the Spirit in his cap; and begged him to be covered.

"What!" exclaimed the Ghost, "would you so soon put out, with worldly hands, the light I give? Is it not enough that you are one of those whose passions made this cap, and force me through whole trains of years to wear it low upon my brow!"

Scrooge reverently disclaimed all intention to offend or any knowledge of having wilfully "bonneted" the Spirit at any period of his life. He then made bold to inquire what business brought him there.

"Your welfare!" said the Ghost.

Scrooge expressed himself much obliged, but could not help thinking that a night of unbroken rest would have been more conducive to that end. The Spirit must have heard him thinking, for it said immediately:

"Your reclamation, then. Take heed!"

It put out its strong hand as it spoke, and clasped him gently by the arm.

"Rise! and walk with me!"

It would have been in vain for Scrooge to plead that the weather and the hour were not adapted to pedestrian purposes; that bed was warm, and the thermometer a long way below freezing; that he was clad but lightly in his slippers, dressing-gown, and nightcap; and that he had a cold upon him at that time. The grasp, though gentle as a woman's hand, was not to be resisted. He rose: but finding that the Spirit made towards the window, clasped his robe in supplication.

"I am a mortal," Scrooge remonstrated, "and liable to fall."

"Bear but a touch of my hand *there*," said the Spirit, laying it upon his heart, "and you shall be upheld in more than this!"

As the words were spoken, they passed through the wall, and stood upon an open country road, with fields on either hand. The city had entirely vanished. Not a vestige of it was to be seen. The darkness and the mist had vanished with it, for it was a clear, cold, winter day, with snow upon the ground.

"Good Heaven!" said Scrooge, clasping his hands together, as he looked about him. "I was bred in this place. I was a boy here!"

The Spirit gazed upon him mildly. Its gentle touch, though it had been light and instantaneous, appeared still present to the old man's sense of feeling. He was conscious of a thousand odours floating in the air, each one connected with a thousand thoughts, and hopes, and joys, and cares long, long, forgotten!

"Your lip is trembling," said the Ghost. "And what is that upon your cheek?"

Scrooge muttered, with an unusual catching in his voice, that it was a pimple; and begged the Ghost to lead him where he would.

"You recollect the way?" inquired the Spirit.

"Remember it!" cried Scrooge with fervour; "I could walk it blindfold."

"Strange to have forgotten it for so many years!" observed the Ghost. "Let us go on."

They walked along the road, Scrooge recognising every gate, and post, and tree; until a little market-town appeared in the distance, with its bridge, its church, and winding river. Some shaggy ponies now were seen trotting towards them with boys upon their backs, who called to other boys in country gigs and carts, driven by farmers. All these boys were in great spirits, and shouted to each other, until the broad fields were so full of merry music, that the crisp air laughed to hear it!

"These are but shadows of the things that have been," said the Ghost. "They have no consciousness of us."

The jocund travellers came on; and as they came, Scrooge knew and named them every one. Why was he rejoiced beyond all bounds to see them! Why did his cold eye glisten, and his heart leap up as they went past! Why was he filled with gladness when he heard them give each other Merry Christmas, as they parted at cross-roads and bye-ways, for their several homes! What was merry Christmas to Scrooge? Out upon merry Christmas! What good had it ever done to him?

"The school is not quite deserted," said the Ghost. "A solitary child, neglected by his friends, is left there still."

Scrooge said he knew it. And he sobbed.

They left the high-road, by a well-remembered lane, and soon approached a mansion of dull red brick, with a little weathercock-surmounted cupola, on the roof, and a bell hanging in it. It was a large house, but one of broken fortunes; for the spacious offices were little used, their walls were damp and mossy, their windows broken, and their gates decayed. Fowls clucked and strutted in the stables; and the coach-houses and sheds were over-run with grass. Nor was it more retentive of its ancient state, within; for entering the dreary hall, and glancing through the open doors of many rooms, they found them poorly furnished, cold, and vast. There was an earthy savour in the air, a chilly bareness in the place, which associated itself somehow with too much getting up by candle-light, and not too much to eat.

They went, the Ghost and Scrooge, across the hall, to a door at the back of the house. It opened before them, and disclosed a long, bare, melancholy room, made barer still by lines of plain deal forms and desks. At one of these a lonely boy was reading near a feeble fire; and Scrooge sat down upon a form, and wept to see his poor forgotten self as he used to be.

Not a latent echo in the house, not a squeak and scuffle from the mice behind the panelling, not a drip from the half-thawed water-spout in the dull yard behind, not a sigh among the leafless boughs of one despondent poplar, not the idle swinging of an empty store-house door, no, not a clicking in the fire, but fell upon the heart of Scrooge with a softening influence, and gave a freer passage to his tears.

The Spirit touched him on the arm, and pointed to his younger self, intent upon his reading. Suddenly a man, in foreign garments: wonderfully real and distinct to look at: stood outside the window, with an axe stuck in his belt, and leading by the bridle an ass laden with wood.

"Why, it's Ali Baba!" Scrooge exclaimed in ecstasy. "It's dear old honest Ali Baba! Yes, yes, I know! One Christmas time, when yonder solitary child was left here all alone, he *did* come, for the first time, just like that. Poor boy! And Valentine," said Scrooge, "and his wild brother, Orson; there they go! And what's his name, who was put down in his drawers, asleep, at the Gate of Damascus; don't you see him! And the Sultan's Groom turned upside down by the Genii; there he is upon his head! Serve him right. I'm glad of it. What business had *he* to be married to the Princess!"

To hear Scrooge expending all the earnestness of his nature on such subjects, in a most extraordinary voice between laughing and crying; and to see his heightened and excited face; would have been a surprise to his business friends in the city, indeed.

"There's the Parrot!" cried Scrooge. "Green body and yellow tail, with a thing like a lettuce growing out of the top of his head; there he is! Poor Robin Crusoe, he called him, when he came home again after sailing round the island. 'Poor Robin Crusoe, where have you been, Robin Crusoe?' The man thought he was dreaming, but he wasn't. It was the Parrot, you know. There goes Friday, running for his life to the little creek! Halloa! Hoop! Halloo!"

Then, with a rapidity of transition very foreign to his usual character, he said, in pity for his former self, "Poor boy!" and cried again.

"I wish," Scrooge muttered, putting his hand in his pocket, and looking about him, after drying his eyes with his cuff: "but it's too late now."

"What is the matter?" asked the Spirit.

"Nothing," said Scrooge. "Nothing. There was a boy singing a Christmas Carol at my door last night. I should like to have given him something: that's all."

The Ghost smiled thoughtfully, and waved its hand: saying as it did so, "Let us see another Christmas!"

Scrooge's former self grew larger at the words, and the room became a little darker and more dirty. The panels shrunk, the windows cracked; fragments of plaster fell out of the ceiling, and the naked laths were shown instead; but how all this was brought about, Scrooge knew no more than you do. He only knew that it was quite correct; that everything had happened so; that there he was, alone again, when all the other boys had gone home for the jolly holidays.

He was not reading now, but walking up and down despairingly. Scrooge looked at the Ghost, and with a mournful shaking of his head, glanced anxiously towards the door.

It opened; and a little girl, much younger than the boy, came darting in, and putting her arms about his neck, and often kissing him, addressed him as her "Dear, dear brother."

"I have come to bring you home, dear brother!" said the child, clapping her tiny hands, and bending down to laugh. "To bring you home, home, home!"

"Home, little Fan?" returned the boy.

"Yes!" said the child, brimful of glee. "Home, for good and all. Home, for ever and ever. Father is so much kinder than he used to be, that home's like Heaven! He spoke so gently to me one dear night when I was going to bed, that I was not afraid to ask him once more if you might come home; and he said Yes, you should; and sent me in a coach to bring you. And you're to be a man!" said the child, opening her eyes, "and are never to come back here; but first, we're to be together all the Christmas long, and have the merriest time in all the world."

"You are quite a woman, little Fan!" exclaimed the boy.

She clapped her hands and laughed, and tried to touch his head; but being too little, laughed again, and stood on tiptoe to embrace him. Then she began to drag him, in her childish eagerness, towards the door; and he, nothing loth to go, accompanied her.

A terrible voice in the hall cried, "Bring down Master Scrooge's box, there!" and in the hall appeared the schoolmaster himself, who glared on Master Scrooge with a ferocious condescension, and threw him into a dreadful state of mind by shaking hands with him. He then conveyed him and his sister into the veriest old well of a shivering best-parlour that ever was seen, where the maps upon the wall, and the celestial and terrestrial globes in the windows, were waxy with cold. Here he produced a decanter of curiously light wine, and a block of curiously heavy cake, and administered instalments of those dainties to the young people: at the same time, sending out a meagre servant to offer a glass of "something" to the post-boy, who answered that he thanked the gentleman, but if it was the same tap as he had tasted before, he had rather not. Master Scrooge's trunk being by this time tied on to the top of the chaise, the children bade the schoolmaster good-bye right willingly; and getting into it, drove gaily down the garden-sweep: the quick wheels dashing the hoar-frost and snow from off the dark leaves of the evergreens like spray.

"Always a delicate creature, whom a breath might have withered," said the Ghost. "But she had a large heart!"

"So she had," cried Scrooge. "You're right. I will not gainsay it, Spirit. God forbid!"

"She died a woman," said the Ghost, "and had, as I think, children."

"One child," Scrooge returned.

"True," said the Ghost. "Your nephew!"

Scrooge seemed uneasy in his mind; and answered briefly, "Yes."

Although they had but that moment left the school behind them, they were now in the busy thoroughfares of a city, where shadowy passengers passed and repassed; where shadowy carts and coaches battled for the way, and all the strife and tumult of a real city were. It was made plain enough, by the dressing of the shops, that here too it was Christmas time again; but it was evening, and the streets were lighted up.

The Ghost stopped at a certain warehouse door, and asked Scrooge if he knew it.

"Know it!" said Scrooge. "Was I apprenticed here!"

They went in. At sight of an old gentleman in a Welsh wig, sitting behind such a high desk, that if he had been two inches taller he must have knocked his head against the ceiling, Scrooge cried in great excitement:

"Why, it's old Fezziwig! Bless his heart; it's Fezziwig alive again!"

Old Fezziwig laid down his pen, and looked up

at the clock, which pointed to the hour of seven. He rubbed his hands; adjusted his capacious waistcoat; laughed all over himself, from his shoes to his organ of benevolence; and called out in a comfortable, oily, rich, fat, jovial voice:

"Yo ho, there! Ebenezer! Dick!"

Scrooge's former self, now grown a young man, came briskly in, accompanied by his fellow-'prentice.

"Dick Wilkins, to be sure!" said Scrooge to the Ghost. "Bless me, yes. There he is. He was very much attached to me, was Dick. Poor Dick! Dear, dear!"

"Yo ho, my boys!" said Fezziwig. "No more work to-night. Christmas Eve, Dick. Christmas, Ebenezer! Let's have the shutters up," cried old Fezziwig, with a sharp clap of his hands, "before a man can say Jack Robinson!"

You wouldn't believe how those two fellows went at it! They charged into the street with the shutters—one, two, three—had 'em up in their places—four, five, six—barred 'em and pinned 'em—seven, eight, nine—and came back before you could have got to twelve, panting like race-horses.

"Hilli-ho!" cried old Fezziwig, skipping down

from the high desk, with wonderful agility. "Clear away, my lads, and let's have lots of room here! Hilli-ho, Dick! Chirrup, Ebenezer!"

Clear away! There was nothing they wouldn't have cleared away, or couldn't have cleared away, with old Fezziwig looking on. It was done in a minute. Every movable was packed off, as if it were dismissed from public life for evermore; the floor was swept and watered, the lamps were trimmed, fuel was heaped upon the fire; and the warehouse was as snug, and warm, and dry, and bright a ball-room, as you would desire to see upon a winter's night.

In came a fiddler with a music-book, and went up to the lofty desk, and made an orchestra of it, and tuned like fifty stomach-aches. In came Mrs. Fezziwig, one vast substantial smile. In came the three Miss Fezziwigs, beaming and lovable. In came the six young followers whose hearts they broke. In came all the young men and women employed in the business. In came the housemaid, with her cousin, the baker. In came the cook, with her brother's particular friend, the milkman. In came the boy from over the way, who was suspected of not having board enough from his master; trying to hide himself behind the girl from next door but one, who was proved to have had her ears pulled by her mistress. In they all came, one after another; some shyly, some boldly, some gracefully, some awkwardly, some pushing, some pulling; in they all came, anyhow and everyhow. Away they all went, twenty couple at once; hands half round and back again the other way; down the middle and up again; round and round in various stages of affectionate grouping; old top couple always turning up in the wrong place; new top couple starting off again, as soon as they got there; all top couples at last, and not a bottom one to help them! When this result was brought about, old Fezziwig, clapping his hands to stop the dance, cried out, "Well done!" and the fiddler plunged his hot face into a pot of porter, especially provided for that purpose. But scorning rest, upon his reappearance, he instantly began again, though there were no dancers yet, as if the other fiddler had been carried home, exhausted, on a shutter, and he were a bran-new man resolved to beat him out of sight, or perish.

There were more dances, and there were forfeits,

and more dances, and there was cake, and there was negus, and there was a great piece of Cold Roast, and there was a great piece of Cold Boiled, and there were mince-pies, and plenty of beer. But the great effect of the evening came after the Roast and Boiled, when the fiddler (an artful dog, mind! The sort of man who knew his business better than you or I could have told it him!) struck up "Sir Roger de Coverley." Then old Fezziwig stood out to dance with Mrs. Fezziwig. Top couple, too; with a good stiff piece of work cut out for them; three or four and twenty pair of partners; people who were not to be trifled with; people who *would* dance, and had no notion of walking.

But if they had been twice as many—ah, four times—old Fezziwig would have been a match for them, and so would Mrs. Fezziwig. As to *her*, she was worthy to be his partner in every sense of the term. If that's not high praise, tell me higher, and I'll use it. A positive light appeared to issue from Fezziwig's calves. They shone in every part of the dance like moons. You couldn't have predicted, at any given time, what would have become of them next. And when old Fezziwig and Mrs. Fezziwig had gone all through the dance; advance and retire, both hands to your partner, bow and curtsey, corkscrew, thread-the-needle, and back again to your place; Fezziwig "cut"—cut so deftly, that he appeared to wink with his legs, and came upon his feet again without a stagger.

When the clock struck eleven, this domestic ball broke up. Mr. and Mrs. Fezziwig took their stations, one on either side of the door, and shaking hands with every person individually as he or she went out, wished him or her a Merry Christmas. When everybody had retired but the two 'prentices, they did the same to them; and thus the cheerful voices died away, and the lads were left to their beds; which were under a counter in the back-shop.

During the whole of this time, Scrooge had acted like a man out of his wits. His heart and soul were in the scene, and with his former self. He corroborated everything, remembered everything, enjoyed everything, and underwent the strangest agitation. It was not until now, when the bright faces of his former self and Dick were turned from them, that he remembered the Ghost, and became conscious that it was looking full upon him, while the light upon its head burnt very clear.

"A small matter," said the Ghost, "to make these silly folks so full of gratitude."

"Small!" echoed Scrooge.

The Spirit signed to him to listen to the two apprentices, who were pouring out their hearts in praise of Fezziwig: and when he had done so, said,

"Why! Is it not? He has spent but a few pounds of your mortal money: three or four perhaps. Is that so much that he deserves this praise?"

"It isn't that," said Scrooge, heated by the remark, and speaking unconsciously like his former, not his latter, self. "It isn't that, Spirit. He has the power to render us happy or unhappy; to make our service light or burdensome; a pleasure or a toil. Say that his power lies in words and looks; in things so slight and insignificant that it is impossible to add and count 'em up: what then? The happiness he gives, is quite as great as if it cost a fortune."

He felt the Spirit's glance, and stopped.

"What is the matter?" asked the Ghost.

"Nothing particular," said Scrooge.

"Something, I think?" the Ghost insisted.

"No," said Scrooge, "No. I should like to be able to say a word or two to my clerk just now. That's all."

His former self turned down the lamps as he gave utterance to the wish; and Scrooge and the Ghost again stood side by side in the open air.

"My time grows short," observed the Spirit. "Quick!"

This was not addressed to Scrooge, or to any one whom he could see, but it produced an immediate effect. For again Scrooge saw himself. He was older now; a man in the prime of life. His face had not the harsh and rigid lines of later years; but it had begun to wear the signs of care and avarice. There was an eager, greedy, restless motion in the eye, which showed the passion that had taken root, and where the shadow of the growing tree would fall.

He was not alone, but sat by the side of a fair young girl in a mourning-dress: in whose eyes there were tears, which sparkled in the light that shone out of the Ghost of Christmas Past.

"It matters little," she said, softly. "To you, very

little. Another idol has displaced me; and if it can cheer and comfort you in time to come, as I would have tried to do, I have no just cause to grieve."

"What Idol has displaced you?" he rejoined.

"A golden one."

"This is the even-handed dealing of the world!" he said. "There is nothing on which it is so hard as poverty; and there is nothing it professes to condemn with such severity as the pursuit of wealth!"

"You fear the world too much," she answered, gently. "All your other hopes have merged into the hope of being beyond the chance of its sordid reproach. I have seen your nobler aspirations fall off one by one, until the master-passion, Gain, engrosses you. Have I not?"

"What then?" he retorted. "Even if I have grown so much wiser, what then? I am not changed towards you."

She shook her head.

"Am I?"

"Our contract is an old one. It was made when we were both poor and content to be so, until, in good season, we could improve our worldly fortune by our patient industry. You *are* changed. When it was made, you were another man."

"I was a boy," he said impatiently.

"Your own feeling tells you that you were not what you are," she returned. "I am. That which promised happiness when we were one in heart, is fraught with misery now that we are two. How often and how keenly I have thought of this, I will not say. It is enough that I *have* thought of it, and can release you."

"Have I ever sought release?"

"In words. No. Never."

"In what, then?"

"In a changed nature; in an altered spirit; in another atmosphere of life; another Hope as its great end. In everything that made my love of any worth or value in your sight. If this had never been between us," said the girl, looking mildly, but with steadiness, upon him; "tell me, would you seek me out and try to win me now? Ah, no!"

He seemed to yield to the justice of this supposition, in spite of himself. But he said with a struggle, "You think not."

"I would gladly think otherwise if I could," she

answered, "Heaven knows! When *I* have learned a Truth like this, I know how strong and irresistible it must be. But if you were free to-day, to-morrow, yesterday, can even I believe that you would choose a dowerless girl—you who, in your very confidence with her, weigh everything by Gain: or, choosing her, if for a moment you were false enough to your one guiding principle to do so, do I not know that your repentance and regret would surely follow? I do; and I release you. With a full heart, for the love of him you once were."

He was about to speak; but with her head turned from him, she resumed.

"You may—the memory of what is past half makes me hope you will—have pain in this. A very, very brief time, and you will dismiss the recollection of it, gladly, as an unprofitable dream, from which it happened well that you awoke. May you be happy in the life you have chosen!"

She left him, and they parted.

"Spirit!" said Scrooge, "show me no more! Conduct me home. Why do you delight to torture me?"

"One shadow more!" exclaimed the Ghost.

"No more!" cried Scrooge. "No more. I don't wish to see it. Show me no more!"

But the relentless Ghost pinioned him in both his arms, and forced him to observe what happened next.

They were in another scene and place; a room, not very large or handsome, but full of comfort. Near to the winter fire sat a beautiful young girl, so like that last that Scrooge believed it was the same, until he saw *her*, now a comely matron, sitting opposite her daughter. The noise in this room was perfectly tumultuous, for there were more children there than Scrooge in his agitated state of mind could count; and, unlike the celebrated herd in the poem, they were not forty children conducting themselves like one, but every child was conducting itself like forty. The consequences were uproarious beyond belief; but no one seemed to care; on the contrary, the mother and daughter laughed heartily, and enjoyed it very much; and the latter, soon beginning to mingle in the sports, got pillaged by the young brigands most ruthlessly. What would I not have given to be one of them! Though I never could have been so rude, no, no! I wouldn't for the wealth of all the world have crushed that braided hair, and torn it down; and for the precious little shoe, I wouldn't have plucked it off, God bless my soul! to save my life. As to measuring her waist in sport, as they did, bold young brood, I couldn't have done it; I should have expected my arm to have grown round it for a punishment, and never come straight again. And yet I should have dearly liked, I own, to have touched her lips; to have questioned her, that she might have opened them; to have looked upon the lashes of her downcast eyes, and never raised a blush; to have let loose waves of hair, an inch of which would be a keepsake beyond price: in short, I should have liked, I do confess, to have had the lightest licence of a child, and yet to have been man enough to know its value.

But now a knocking at the door was heard, and such a rush immediately ensued that she with laughing face and plundered dress was borne towards it in the centre of a flushed and boisterous group, just in time to greet the father, who came home attended by a man laden with Christmas toys and presents. Then the shouting and the struggling, and the onslaught that was made on the defenceless porter! The scaling him with chairs for ladders to dive into his pockets, despoil him of brown-paper parcels, hold on tight by his cravat, hug him round his neck, pommel his back, and kick his legs in irrepressible affection! The shouts of wonder and delight with which the development of every package was received! The terrible announcement that the baby had been taken in the act of putting a doll's frying-pan into his mouth, and was more than suspected of having swallowed a fictitious turkey, glued on a wooden platter! The immense relief of finding this a false alarm! The joy, and gratitude, and ecstasy! They are all indescribable alike. It is enough that by degrees the children and their emotions got out of the parlour, and by one stair at a time, up to the top of the house; where they went to bed, and so subsided.

And now Scrooge looked on more attentively than ever, when the master of the house, having his daughter leaning fondly on him, sat down with her and her mother at his own fireside; and when he thought that such another creature, quite as graceful and as full of promise, might have called him father, and been a spring-time in the haggard winter of his life, his sight grew very dim indeed.

"Belle," said the husband, turning to his wife with a smile, "I saw an old friend of yours this afternoon."

"Who was it?"

"Guess!"

"How can I? Tut, don't I know?" she added in the same breath, laughing as he laughed. "Mr. Scrooge."

"Mr. Scrooge it was. I passed his office window; and as it was not shut up, and he had a candle inside, I could scarcely help seeing him. His partner lies upon the point of death, I hear; and there he sat alone. Quite alone in the world, I do believe."

"Spirit!" said Scrooge in a broken voice, "remove me from this place."

"I told you these were shadows of the things that have been," said the Ghost. "That they are what they are, do not blame me!"

"Remove me!" Scrooge exclaimed, "I cannot bear it!"

He turned upon the Ghost, and seeing that it looked upon him with a face, in which in some strange way there were fragments of all the faces it had shown him, wrestled with it.

"Leave me! Take me back. Haunt me no longer!"

In the struggle, if that can be called a struggle in which the Ghost with no visible resistance on its own part was undisturbed by any effort of its adversary, Scrooge observed that its light was burning high and bright; and dimly connecting that with its influence over him, he seized the extinguisher-cap, and by a sudden action pressed it down upon its head.

The Spirit dropped beneath it, so that the extinguisher covered its whole form; but though Scrooge pressed it down with all his force, he could not hide the light: which streamed from under it, in an unbroken flood upon the ground.

He was conscious of being exhausted, and overcome by an irresistible drowsiness; and, further, of being in his own bedroom. He gave the cap a parting squeeze, in which his hand relaxed; and had barely time to reel to bed, before he sank into a heavy sleep.

## Stave Three

# THE SECOND OF THE THREE SPIRITS

Awaking in the middle of a prodigiously tough snore, and sitting up in bed to get his thoughts together,

Scrooge had no occasion to be told that the bell was again upon the stroke of One. He felt that he was restored to consciousness in the right nick of time, for the especial purpose of holding a conference with the second messenger despatched to him through Jacob Marley's intervention. But finding that he turned uncomfortably cold when he began to wonder which of his curtains this new spectre would draw back, he put them every one aside with his own hands; and lying down again, established a sharp look-out all round the bed. For he wished to challenge the Spirit on the moment of its appearance, and did not wish to be taken by surprise, and made nervous.

Gentlemen of the free-and-easy sort, who plume themselves on being acquainted with a move or two, and being usually equal to the time-of-day, express the wide range of their capacity for adventure by observing that they are good for anything from pitch-and-toss to manslaughter; between which opposite extremes, no doubt, there lies a tolerably wide and comprehensive range of subjects. Without venturing for Scrooge quite as hardily as this, I don't mind calling on you to believe that he was ready for a good broad field of strange appearances, and that nothing between a baby and rhinoceros would have astonished him very much.

Now, being prepared for almost anything, he was not by any means prepared for nothing; and, consequently, when the Bell struck One, and no shape appeared, he was taken with a violent fit of trembling. Five minutes, ten minutes, a quarter of an hour went by, yet nothing came. All this time, he lay upon his bed, the very core and centre of a blaze of ruddy light, which streamed upon it when the clock proclaimed the hour; and which, being only light, was more alarming than a dozen ghosts, as he was powerless to make out what it meant, or would be at; and was sometimes apprehensive that he might be at that very moment an interesting case of spontaneous combustion, without having the consolation of knowing it. At last, however, he began to think—as you or I would have thought at first; for it is always the person not in the predicament who knows what ought to have been done in it, and would unquestionably have done it too—at last, I say, he began to think that the source and secret of this ghostly light might be in the adjoining room, from whence, on further tracing it, it seemed to shine. This idea taking full possession of his mind, he got up softly and shuffled in his slippers to the door.

The moment Scrooge's hand was on the lock, a strange voice called him by his name, and bade him enter. He obeyed.

It was his own room. There was no doubt about that. But it had undergone a surprising transformation. The walls and ceiling were so hung with living green, that it looked a perfect grove; from every part of which, bright gleaming berries glistened. The crisp leaves of holly, mistletoe, and ivy reflected back the light, as if so many little mirrors had been scattered there; and such a mighty blaze went roaring up the chimney, as that dull petrification of a hearth had never known in Scrooge's time, or Marley's, or for many and many a winter season gone. Heaped up on the floor, to form a kind of throne, were turkeys, geese, game, poultry, brawn, great joints of meat, sucking-pigs, long wreaths of sausages, mince-pies, plum-puddings, barrels of oysters, red-hot chestnuts, cherry-cheeked apples, juicy oranges, luscious pears, immense twelfth-cakes, and seething bowls of punch, that made the chamber dim with their delicious steam. In easy state upon this couch, there sat a jolly Giant, glorious to see; who bore a glowing torch, in shape not unlike Plenty's horn, and held it up, high up, to shed its light on Scrooge, as he came peeping round the door.

"Come in!" exclaimed the Ghost. "Come in! and know me better, man!"

Scrooge entered timidly, and hung his head before this Spirit. He was not the dogged Scrooge he had been; and though the Spirit's eyes were clear and kind, he did not like to meet them.

"I am the Ghost of Christmas Present," said the Spirit. "Look upon me!"

Scrooge reverently did so. It was clothed in one simple green robe, or mantle, bordered with white fur. This garment hung so loosely on the figure, that its capacious breast was bare, as if disdaining to be warded or concealed by any artifice. Its feet, observable beneath the ample folds of the garment, were also bare; and on its head it wore no other covering than a holly wreath, set here and there with shining icicles. Its dark brown curls were long and free; free as its genial face, its sparkling eye, its open hand, its cheery voice, its unconstrained demeanour, and its joyful air. Girded round its middle was an antique scabbard; but no sword was in it, and the ancient sheath was eaten up with rust.

"You have never seen the like of me before!" exclaimed the Spirit.

"Never," Scrooge made answer to it.

"Have never walked forth with the younger members of my family; meaning (for I am very young) my elder brothers born in these later years?" pursued the Phantom.

"I don't think I have," said Scrooge. "I am afraid I have not. Have you had many brothers, Spirit?"

"More than eighteen hundred," said the Ghost.

"A tremendous family to provide for!" muttered Scrooge.

The Ghost of Christmas Present rose.

"Spirit," said Scrooge submissively, "conduct me where you will. I went forth last night on compulsion, and I learnt a lesson which is working now. To-night, if you have aught to teach me, let me profit by it."

"Touch my robe!"

Scrooge did as he was told, and held it fast.

Holly, mistletoe, red berries, ivy, turkeys, geese, game, poultry, brawn, meat, pigs, sausages, oysters, pies, puddings, fruit, and punch, all vanished instantly. So did the room, the fire, the ruddy glow, the hour of night, and they stood in the city streets on Christmas morning, where (for the weather was severe) the people made a rough, but brisk and not unpleasant kind of music, in scraping the snow from the pavement in front of their dwellings, and from the tops of their houses, whence it was mad delight to the boys to see it come plumping down into the road below, and splitting into artificial little snow-storms.

The house fronts looked black enough, and the windows blacker, contrasting with the smooth white sheet of snow upon the roofs, and with the dirtier snow upon the ground; which last deposit had been ploughed up in deep furrows by the heavy wheels of carts and waggons; furrows that crossed and re-crossed each other hundreds of times where the great streets branched off; and made intricate channels, hard to trace in the thick yellow mud and icy water.

The sky was gloomy, and the shortest streets were choked up with a dingy mist, half thawed, half frozen, whose heavier particles descended in a shower of sooty atoms, as if all the chimneys in Great Britain had, by one consent, caught fire, and were blazing away to their dear hearts' content. There was nothing very cheerful in the climate or the town, and yet was there an air of cheerfulness abroad that the clearest summer air and brightest summer sun might have endeavoured to diffuse in vain.

For, the people who were shovelling away on the housetops were jovial and full of glee; calling out to one another from the parapets, and now and then exchanging a facetious snowball—better-natured missile far than many a wordy jest—laughing heartily if it went right and not less heartily if it went wrong. The poulterers' shops were still half open, and the fruiterers' were radiant in their glory. There were great, round, pot-bellied baskets of chestnuts, shaped like the waistcoats of jolly old gentlemen, lolling at the doors, and tumbling out into the street in their apoplectic opulence. There were ruddy, brown-faced, broad-girthed Spanish Onions, shining in the fatness of their growth like Spanish Friars, and winking from their shelves in wanton slyness at the girls as they went by, and glanced demurely at the hung-up mistletoe. There were pears and apples, clustered high in blooming pyramids; there were bunches of grapes, made, in the shopkeepers' benevolence to dangle from conspicuous hooks, that people's mouths might water gratis as they passed; there were piles of filberts, mossy and brown, recalling, in their fragrance, ancient walks among the woods, and pleasant shufflings ankle deep through withered leaves; there were Norfolk Biffins, squat and swarthy, setting off the yellow of the oranges and lemons, and, in the great compactness of their juicy persons, urgently entreating and beseeching to be carried home in paper bags and eaten after dinner. The very gold and silver fish, set forth among these choice fruits in a bowl, though members of a dull and stagnant-blooded race, appeared to know that there was something going on; and, to a fish, went gasping round and round their little world in slow and passionless excitement.

The Grocers'! oh, the Grocers'! nearly closed,

with perhaps two shutters down, or one; but through those gaps such glimpses! It was not alone that the scales descending on the counter made a merry sound, or that the twine and roller parted company so briskly, or that the canisters were rattled up and down like juggling tricks, or even that the blended scents of tea and coffee were so grateful to the nose, or even that the raisins were so plentiful and rare, the almonds so extremely white, the sticks of cinnamon so long and straight, the other spices so delicious, the candied fruits so caked and spotted with molten sugar as to make the coldest lookers-on feel faint and subsequently bilious. Nor was it that the figs were moist and pulpy, or that the French plums blushed in modest tartness from their highly deco-rated boxes, or that everything was good to eat and in its Christmas dress; but the customers were all so hurried and so eager in the hopeful promise of the day, that they tumbled up against each other at the door, crashing their wicker baskets wildly, and left their purchases upon the counter, and came running back to fetch them, and committed hundreds of the like mistakes, in the best humour possible; while the

Grocer and his people were so frank and fresh that the polished hearts with which they fastened their aprons behind might have been their own, worn outside for general inspection, and for Christmas daws to peck at if they chose.

But soon the steeples called good people all, to church and chapel, and away they came, flocking through the streets in their best clothes, and with their gayest faces. And at the same time there emerged from scores of bye-streets, lanes, and nameless turnings, innumerable people, carrying their dinners to the bakers' shops. The sight of these poor revellers appeared to interest the Spirit very much, for he stood with Scrooge beside him in a baker's doorway, and taking off the covers as their bearers passed, sprinkled incense on their dinners from his torch. And it was a very uncommon kind of torch, for once or twice when there were angry words between some dinner-carriers who had jostled each other, he shed a few drops of water on them from it, and their good humour was restored directly. For they said, it was a shame to quarrel upon Christmas Day. And so it was! God love it, so it was!

In time the bells ceased, and the bakers were shut up; and yet there was a genial shadowing forth of all these dinners and the progress of their cooking, in the thawed blotch of wet above each baker's oven; where the pavement smoked as if its stones were cooking too.

"Is there a peculiar flavour in what you sprinkle from your torch?" asked Scrooge.

"There is. My own."

"Would it apply to any kind of dinner on this day?" asked Scrooge.

"To any kindly given. To a poor one most."

"Why to a poor one most?" asked Scrooge.

"Because it needs it most."

"Spirit," said Scrooge, after a moment's thought, "I wonder you, of all the beings in the many worlds about us, should desire to cramp these people's opportunities of innocent enjoyment."

"I!" cried the Spirit.

"You would deprive them of their means of dining every seventh day, often the only day on which they can be said to dine at all," said Scrooge. "Wouldn't you?"

"I!" cried the Spirit.

"You seek to close these places on the Seventh Day?" said Scrooge. "And it comes to the same thing."

"*I* seek!" exclaimed the Spirit.

"Forgive me if I am wrong. It has been done in your name, or at least in that of your family," said Scrooge.

"There are some upon this earth of yours," returned the Spirit, "who lay claim to know us, and who do their deeds of passion, pride, ill-will, hatred, envy, bigotry, and selfishness in our name, who are as strange to us and all our kith and kin, as if they had never lived. Remember that, and charge their doings on themselves, not us."

Scrooge promised that he would; and they went on, invisible, as they had been before, into the suburbs of the town. It was a remarkable quality of the Ghost (which Scrooge had observed at the baker's), that notwithstanding his gigantic size, he could accommodate himself to any place with ease; and that he stood beneath a low roof quite as gracefully and like a supernatural creature, as it was possible he could have done in any lofty hall.

And perhaps it was the pleasure the good Spirit had in showing off this power of his, or else it was his own kind, generous, hearty nature, and his sympathy with all poor men, that led him straight to Scrooge's clerk's; for there he went, and took Scrooge with him, holding to his robe; and on the threshold of the door the Spirit smiled, and stopped to bless Bob Cratchit's dwelling with the sprinkling of his torch. Think of that! Bob had but fifteen "Bob" a-week himself; he pocketed on Saturdays but fifteen copies of his Christian name; and yet the Ghost of Christmas Present blessed his four-roomed house!

Then up rose Mrs. Cratchit, Cratchit's wife, dressed out but poorly in a twice-turned gown, but brave in ribbons, which are cheap and make a goodly show for sixpence; and she laid the cloth, assisted by Belinda Cratchit, second of her daughters, also brave in ribbons; while Master Peter Cratchit plunged a fork into the saucepan of potatoes, and getting the corners of his monstrous shirt collar (Bob's private property, conferred upon his son and heir in honour of the day) into his mouth, rejoiced to find himself so gallantly attired, and yearned to show his linen in the fashionable Parks. And now two smaller Cratchits, boy and girl, came tearing in, screaming that outside the baker's they had smelt the goose, and known it for their own; and basking in luxurious thoughts of sage and onion, these young Cratchits danced about the table, and exalted Master Peter Cratchit to the skies, while he (not proud, although his collars nearly choked him) blew the fire, until the slow potatoes bubbling up, knocked loudly at the saucepan-lid to be let out and peeled.

"What has ever got your precious father then?" said Mrs. Cratchit. "And your brother, Tiny Tim! And Martha warn't as late last Christmas Day by half-an-hour?"

"Here's Martha, mother!" said a girl, appearing as she spoke.

"Here's Martha, mother!" cried the two young Cratchits. "Hurrah! There's *such* a goose, Martha!"

"Why, bless your heart alive, my dear, how late you are!" said Mrs. Cratchit, kissing her a dozen times, and taking off her shawl and bonnet for her with officious zeal.

"We'd a deal of work to finish up last night,"

replied the girl, "and had to clear away this morning, mother!"

"Well! Never mind so long as you are come," said Mrs. Cratchit. "Sit ye down before the fire, my dear, and have a warm, Lord bless ye!"

"No, no! There's father coming," cried the two young Cratchits, who were everywhere at once. "Hide, Martha, hide!"

So Martha hid herself, and in came little Bob, the father, with at least three feet of comforter exclusive of the fringe, hanging down before him; and his threadbare clothes darned up and brushed, to look seasonable; and Tiny Tim upon his shoulder. Alas for Tiny Tim, he bore a little crutch, and had his limbs supported by an iron frame!

"Why, where's our Martha?" cried Bob Cratchit, looking round.

"Not coming," said Mrs. Cratchit.

"Not coming!" said Bob, with a sudden declension in his high spirits; for he had been Tim's blood horse all the way from church, and had come home rampant. "Not coming upon Christmas Day!"

Martha didn't like to see him disappointed, if

it were only in joke; so she came out prematurely from behind the closet door, and ran into his arms, while the two young Cratchits hustled Tiny Tim, and bore him off into the wash-house, that he might hear the pudding singing in the copper.

"And how did little Tim behave?" asked Mrs. Cratchit, when she had rallied Bob on his credulity, and Bob had hugged his daughter to his heart's content.

"As good as gold," said Bob, "and better. Somehow he gets thoughtful, sitting by himself so much, and thinks the strangest things you ever heard. He told me, coming home, that he hoped the people saw him in the church, because he was a cripple, and it might be pleasant to them to remember upon Christmas Day, who made lame beggars walk, and blind men see."

Bob's voice was tremulous when he told them this, and trembled more when he said that Tiny Tim was growing strong and hearty.

His active little crutch was heard upon the floor, and back came Tiny Tim before another word was spoken, escorted by his brother and sister to his stool before the fire; and while Bob, turning up his cuffs—as if, poor fellow, they were capable of being made more shabby—compounded some hot mixture in a jug with gin and lemons, and stirred it round and round and put it on the hob to simmer; Master Peter, and the two ubiquitous young Cratchits went to fetch the goose, with which they soon returned in high procession.

Such a bustle ensued that you might have thought a goose the rarest of all birds; a feathered phenomenon, to which a black swan was a matter of course—and in truth it was something very like it in that house. Mrs. Cratchit made the gravy (ready beforehand in a little saucepan) hissing hot; Master Peter mashed the potatoes with incredible vigour; Miss Belinda sweetened up the apple-sauce; Martha dusted the hot plates; Bob took Tiny Tim beside him in a tiny corner at the table; the two young Cratchits set chairs for everybody, not forgetting themselves, and mounting guard upon their posts, crammed spoons into their mouths, lest they should shriek for goose before their turn came to be helped. At last the dishes were set on, and grace was said. It was succeeded by a breathless pause, as Mrs. Cratchit, looking slowly all along the carving-knife, prepared to plunge it in the breast; but when she did, and when the long expected gush of stuffing issued forth, one murmur of delight arose all round the board, and even Tiny Tim, excited by the two young Cratchits, beat on the table with the handle of his knife, and feebly cried Hurrah!

There never was such a goose. Bob said he didn't believe there ever was such a goose cooked. Its tenderness and flavour, size and cheapness, were the themes of universal admiration. Eked out by apple-sauce and mashed potatoes, it was a sufficient dinner for the whole family; indeed, as Mrs. Cratchit said with great delight (surveying one small atom of a bone upon the dish), they hadn't ate it all at last! Yet every one had had enough, and the youngest Cratchits in particular, were steeped in sage and onion to the eyebrows! But now, the plates being changed by Miss Belinda, Mrs. Cratchit left the room alone—too nervous to bear witnesses—to take the pudding up and bring it in.

Suppose it should not be done enough! Suppose

it should break in turning out! Suppose somebody should have got over the wall of the back-yard, and stolen it, while they were merry with the goose—a supposition at which the two young Cratchits became livid! All sorts of horrors were supposed.

Hallo! A great deal of steam! The pudding was out of the copper. A smell like a washing-day! That was the cloth. A smell like an eating-house and a pastrycook's next door to each other, with a laundress's next door to that! That was the pudding! In half a minute Mrs. Cratchit entered—flushed, but smiling proudly—with the pudding, like a speckled cannon-ball, so hard and firm, blazing in half of half-a-quartern of ignited brandy, and bedight with Christmas holly stuck into the top.

Oh, a wonderful pudding! Bob Cratchit said, and calmly too, that he regarded it as the greatest success achieved by Mrs. Cratchit since their marriage. Mrs. Cratchit said that now the weight was off her mind, she would confess she had had her doubts about the quantity of flour. Everybody had something to say about it, but nobody said or thought it was at all a small pudding for a large family. It would have been flat heresy to do so. Any Cratchit would have blushed to hint at such a thing.

At last the dinner was all done, the cloth was cleared, the hearth swept, and the fire made up. The compound in the jug being tasted, and considered perfect, apples and oranges were put upon the table, and a shovel-full of chestnuts on the fire. Then all the Cratchit family drew round the hearth, in what Bob Cratchit called a circle, meaning half a one; and at Bob Cratchit's elbow stood the family display of glass. Two tumblers, and a custard-cup without a handle.

These held the hot stuff from the jug, however, as well as golden goblets would have done; and Bob served it out with beaming looks, while the chestnuts on the fire sputtered and cracked noisily. Then Bob proposed:

"A Merry Christmas to us all, my dears. God bless us!"

Which all the family re-echoed.

"God bless us every one!" said Tiny Tim, the last of all.

He sat very close to his father's side upon his

little stool. Bob held his withered little hand in his, as if he loved the child, and wished to keep him by his side, and dreaded that he might be taken from him.

"Spirit," said Scrooge, with an interest he had never felt before, "tell me if Tiny Tim will live."

"I see a vacant seat," replied the Ghost, "in the poor chimney-corner, and a crutch without an owner, carefully preserved. If these shadows remain unaltered by the Future, the child will die."

"No, no," said Scrooge. "Oh, no, kind Spirit! say he will be spared."

"If these shadows remain unaltered by the Future, none other of my race," returned the Ghost, "will find him here. What then? If he be like to die, he had better do it, and decrease the surplus population."

Scrooge hung his head to hear his own words quoted by the Spirit, and was overcome with penitence and grief.

"Man," said the Ghost, "if man you be in heart, not adamant, forbear that wicked cant until you have discovered What the surplus is, and Where it is. Will you decide what men shall live, what men shall die? It may be, that in the sight of Heaven, you are more worthless and less fit to live than millions like this poor man's child. Oh God! to hear the Insect on the leaf pronouncing on the too much life among his hungry brothers in the dust!"

Scrooge bent before the Ghost's rebuke, and trembling cast his eyes upon the ground. But he raised them speedily, on hearing his own name.

"Mr. Scrooge!" said Bob; "I'll give you Mr. Scrooge, the Founder of the Feast!"

"The Founder of the Feast indeed!" cried Mrs. Cratchit, reddening. "I wish I had him here. I'd give him a piece of my mind to feast upon, and I hope he'd have a good appetite for it."

"My dear," said Bob, "the children! Christmas Day."

"It should be Christmas Day, I am sure," said she, "on which one drinks the health of such an odious, stingy, hard, unfeeling man as Mr. Scrooge. You know he is, Robert! Nobody knows it better than you do, poor fellow!"

"My dear," was Bob's mild answer, "Christmas Day."

"I'll drink his health for your sake and the Day's,"

said Mrs. Cratchit, "not for his. Long life to him! A merry Christmas and a happy new year! He'll be very merry and very happy, I have no doubt!"

The children drank the toast after her. It was the first of their proceedings which had no heartiness. Tiny Tim drank it last of all, but he didn't care twopence for it. Scrooge was the Ogre of the family. The mention of his name cast a dark shadow on the party, which was not dispelled for full five minutes.

After it had passed away, they were ten times merrier than before, from the mere relief of Scrooge the Baleful being done with. Bob Cratchit told them how he had a situation in his eye for Master Peter, which would bring in, if obtained, full five-and-sixpence weekly. The two young Cratchits laughed tremendously at the idea of Peter's being a man of business; and Peter himself looked thoughtfully at the fire from between his collars, as if he were deliberating what particular investments he should favour when he came into the receipt of that bewildering income. Martha, who was a poor apprentice at a milliner's, then told them what kind of work she had to do, and how many hours she worked at a stretch, and how she meant to lie abed to-morrow morning for a good long rest; to-morrow being a holiday she passed at home. Also how she had seen a countess and a lord some days before, and how the lord "was much about as tall as Peter"; at which Peter pulled up his collars so high that you couldn't have seen his head if you had been there. All this time the chestnuts and the jug went round and round; and by-and-by they had a song, about a lost child travelling in the snow, from Tiny Tim, who had a plaintive little voice, and sang it very well indeed.

There was nothing of high mark in this. They were not a handsome family; they were not well dressed; their shoes were far from being water-proof; their clothes were scanty; and Peter might have known, and very likely did, the inside of a pawn-broker's. But, they were happy, grateful, pleased with one another, and contented with the time; and when they faded, and looked happier yet in the bright sprinklings of the Spirit's torch at parting, Scrooge had his eye upon them, and especially on Tiny Tim, until the last.

By this time it was getting dark, and snowing

pretty heavily; and as Scrooge and the Spirit went along the streets, the brightness of the roaring fires in kitchens, parlours, and all sorts of rooms, was wonderful. Here, the flickering of the blaze showed preparations for a cosy dinner, with hot plates baking through and through before the fire, and deep red curtains, ready to be drawn to shut out cold and darkness. There all the children of the house were running out into the snow to meet their married sisters, brothers, cousins, uncles, aunts, and be the first to greet them. Here, again, were shadows on the window-blind of guests assembling; and there a group of handsome girls, all hooded and fur-booted, and all chattering at once, tripped lightly off to some near neighbour's house; where, woe upon the single man who saw them enter—artful witches, well they knew it—in a glow!

But, if you had judged from the numbers of people on their way to friendly gatherings, you might have thought that no one was at home to give them welcome when they got there, instead of every house expecting company, and piling up its fires half-chimney high. Blessings on it, how the Ghost exulted!

How it bared its breadth of breast, and opened its capacious palm, and floated on, outpouring, with a generous hand, its bright and harmless mirth on everything within its reach! The very lamplighter, who ran on before, dotting the dusky street with specks of light, and who was dressed to spend the evening somewhere, laughed out loudly as the Spirit passed, though little kenned the lamplighter that he had any company but Christmas!

And now, without a word of warning from the Ghost, they stood upon a bleak and desert moor, where monstrous masses of rude stone were cast about, as though it were the burial-place of giants; and water spread itself wheresoever it listed, or would have done so, but for the frost that held it prisoner; and nothing grew but moss and furze, and coarse rank grass. Down in the west the setting sun had left a streak of fiery red, which glared upon the desolation for an instant, like a sullen eye, and frowning lower, lower, lower yet, was lost in the thick gloom of darkest night.

"What place is this?" asked Scrooge.

"A place where Miners live, who labour in the bowels of the earth," returned the Spirit. "But they know me. See!"

A light shone from the window of a hut, and swiftly they advanced towards it. Passing through the wall of mud and stone, they found a cheerful company assembled round a glowing fire. An old, old man and woman, with their children and their children's children, and another generation beyond that, all decked out gaily in their holiday attire. The old man, in a voice that seldom rose above the howling of the wind upon the barren waste, was singing them a Christmas song—it had been a very old song when he was a boy—and from time to time they all joined in the chorus. So surely as they raised their voices, the old man got quite blithe and loud; and so surely as they stopped, his vigour sank again.

The Spirit did not tarry here, but bade Scrooge hold his robe, and passing on above the moor, sped—whither? Not to sea? To sea. To Scrooge's horror, looking back, he saw the last of the land, a frightful range of rocks, behind them; and his ears were deafened by the thundering of water, as it rolled and roared, and raged among the dreadful caverns it had worn, and fiercely tried to undermine the earth.

Built upon a dismal reef of sunken rocks, some league or so from shore, on which the waters chafed and dashed, the wild year through, there stood a solitary lighthouse. Great heaps of sea-weed clung to its base, and storm-birds—born of the wind one might suppose, as sea-weed of the water—rose and fell about it, like the waves they skimmed.

But even here, two men who watched the light had made a fire, that through the loophole in the thick stone wall shed out a ray of brightness on the awful sea. Joining their horny hands over the rough table at which they sat, they wished each other Merry Christmas in their can of grog; and one of them: the elder, too, with his face all damaged and scarred with hard weather, as the figure-head of an old ship might be: struck up a sturdy song that was like a Gale in itself.

Again the Ghost sped on, above the black and heaving sea—on, on—until, being far away, as he told Scrooge, from any shore, they lighted on a ship. They stood beside the helmsman at the wheel, the look-out in the bow, the officers who had the watch; dark, ghostly figures in their several stations; but every man among them hummed a Christmas tune, or had a Christmas thought, or spoke below his breath to his companion of some bygone Christmas Day, with homeward hopes belonging to it. And every man on board, waking or sleeping, good or bad, had had a kinder word for another on that day than on any day in the year; and had shared to some extent in its festivities; and had remembered those he cared for at a distance, and had known that they delighted to remember him.

It was a great surprise to Scrooge, while listening to the moaning of the wind, and thinking what a solemn thing it was to move on through the lonely darkness over an unknown abyss, whose depths were secrets as profound as Death: it was a great surprise to Scrooge, while thus engaged, to hear a hearty laugh. It was a much greater surprise to Scrooge to recognise it as his own nephew's and to find himself in a bright, dry, gleaming room, with the Spirit standing smiling by his side, and looking at that same nephew with approving affability!

"Ha, ha!" laughed Scrooge's nephew. "Ha, ha, ha!"

If you should happen, by any unlikely chance, to know a man more blest in a laugh than Scrooge's nephew, all I can say is, I should like to know him too. Introduce him to me, and I'll cultivate his acquaintance.

It is a fair, even-handed, noble adjustment of things, that while there is infection in disease and sorrow, there is nothing in the world so irresistibly contagious as laughter and good-humour. When Scrooge's nephew laughed in this way: holding his sides, rolling his head, and twisting his face into the most extravagant contortions: Scrooge's niece, by marriage, laughed as heartily as he. And their assembled friends being not a bit behindhand, roared out lustily.

"Ha, ha! Ha, ha, ha, ha!"

"He said that Christmas was a humbug, as I live!" cried Scrooge's nephew. "He believed it too!"

"More shame for him, Fred!" said Scrooge's niece, indignantly. Bless those women; they never do anything by halves. They are always in earnest.

She was very pretty: exceedingly pretty. With a dimpled, surprised-looking, capital face; a ripe little mouth, that seemed made to be kissed—as no doubt it was; all kinds of good little dots about her chin, that melted into one another when she laughed; and the sunniest pair of eyes you ever saw in any little creature's head. Altogether she was what you would have called provoking, you know; but satisfactory, too. Oh, perfectly satisfactory.

"He's a comical old fellow," said Scrooge's nephew, "that's the truth: and not so pleasant as he might be. However, his offences carry their own punishment, and I have nothing to say against him."

"I'm sure he is very rich, Fred," hinted Scrooge's niece. "At least you always tell *me* so."

"What of that, my dear!" said Scrooge's nephew. "His wealth is of no use to him. He don't do any good with it. He don't make himself comfortable with it. He hasn't the satisfaction of thinking—ha, ha, ha!— that he is ever going to benefit Us with it."

"I have no patience with him," observed Scrooge's niece. Scrooge's niece's sisters, and all the other ladies, expressed the same opinion.

"Oh, I have!" said Scrooge's nephew. "I am sorry for him; I couldn't be angry with him if I tried. Who suffers by his ill whims! Himself, always. Here, he takes it into his head to dislike us, and he won't come and dine with us. What's the consequence? He don't lose much of a dinner."

"Indeed, I think he loses a very good dinner," interrupted Scrooge's niece. Everybody else said the same, and they must be allowed to have been competent judges, because they had just had dinner; and, with the dessert upon the table, were clustered round the fire, by lamplight.

"Well! I'm very glad to hear it," said Scrooge's nephew, "because I haven't great faith in these young housekeepers. What do *you* say, Topper?"

Topper had clearly got his eye upon one of Scrooge's niece's sisters, for he answered that a bachelor was a wretched outcast, who had no right to express an opinion on the subject. Whereat Scrooge's niece's sister—the plump one with the lace tucker: not the one with the roses—blushed.

"Do go on, Fred," said Scrooge's niece, clapping her hands. "He never finishes what he begins to say! He is such a ridiculous fellow!"

Scrooge's nephew revelled in another laugh, and

as it was impossible to keep the infection off; though the plump sister tried hard to do it with aromatic vinegar; his example was unanimously followed.

"I was only going to say," said Scrooge's nephew, "that the consequence of his taking a dislike to us, and not making merry with us, is, as I think, that he loses some pleasant moments, which could do him no harm. I am sure he loses pleasanter companions than he can find in his own thoughts, either in his mouldy old office, or his dusty chambers. I mean to give him the same chance every year, whether he likes it or not, for I pity him. He may rail at Christmas till he dies, but he can't help thinking better of it—I defy him—if he finds me going there, in good temper, year after year, and saying Uncle Scrooge, how are you? If it only puts him in the vein to leave his poor clerk fifty pounds, *that's* something; and I think I shook him yesterday."

It was their turn to laugh now at the notion of his shaking Scrooge. But being thoroughly good-natured, and not much caring what they laughed at, so that they laughed at any rate, he encouraged them in their merriment, and passed the bottle joyously.

After tea, they had some music. For they were a musical family, and knew what they were about, when they sung a Glee or Catch, I can assure you: especially Topper, who could growl away in the bass like a good one, and never swell the large veins in his forehead, or get red in the face over it. Scrooge's niece played well upon the harp; and played among other tunes a simple little air (a mere nothing: you might learn to whistle it in two minutes), which had been familiar to the child who fetched Scrooge from the boarding-school, as he had been reminded by the Ghost of Christmas Past. When this strain of music sounded, all the things that Ghost had shown him, came upon his mind; he softened more and more; and thought that if he could have listened to it often, years ago, he might have cultivated the kindnesses of life for his own happiness with his own hands, without resorting to the sexton's spade that buried Jacob Marley.

But they didn't devote the whole evening to music. After a while they played at forfeits; for it is good to be children sometimes, and never better than at Christmas, when its mighty Founder was a child himself. Stop! There was first a game at blind-man's buff. Of course there was. And I no more believe Topper was really blind than I believe he had eyes in his boots. My opinion is, that it was a done thing between him and Scrooge's nephew; and that the Ghost of Christmas Present knew it. The way he went after that plump sister in the lace tucker was an outrage on the credulity of human nature. Knocking down the fire-irons, tumbling over the chairs, bumping against the piano, smothering himself among the curtains, wherever she went, there went he! He always knew where the plump sister was. He wouldn't catch anybody else. If you had fallen up against him (as some of them did), on purpose, he would have made a feint of endeavouring to seize you, which would have been an affront to your understanding, and would instantly have sidled off in the direction of the plump sister. She often cried out that it wasn't fair; and it really was not. But when at last, he caught her; when, in spite of all her silken rustlings, and her rapid flutterings past him, he got her into a corner whence there was no escape; then his conduct was the most execrable. For his pretending not to know her; his pretending that it was necessary to touch her head-dress, and further to assure himself of her identity by pressing a certain ring upon her finger, and a certain chain about her neck; was vile, monstrous! No doubt she told him her opinion of it, when, another blind-man being in office, they were so very confidential together, behind the curtains.

Scrooge's niece was not one of the blind-man's buff party, but was made comfortable with a large chair and a footstool, in a snug corner, where the Ghost and Scrooge were close behind her. But she joined in the forfeits, and loved her love to admiration with all the letters of the alphabet. Likewise at the game of How, When, and Where, she was very great, and to the secret joy of Scrooge's nephew, beat her sisters hollow: though they were sharp girls too, as Topper could have told you. There might have been twenty people there, young and old, but they all played, and so did Scrooge; for wholly forgetting in the interest he had in what was going on, that his voice made no sound in their ears, he sometimes came out with his guess quite loud, and very often guessed quite right, too; for the sharpest needle, best Whitechapel, warranted not to cut in the eye, was not sharper than Scrooge; blunt as he took it in his head to be.

The Ghost was greatly pleased to find him in this mood, and looked upon him with such favour, that he begged like a boy to be allowed to stay until the guests departed. But this the Spirit said could not be done.

"Here is a new game," said Scrooge. "One half hour, Spirit, only one!"

It was a Game called Yes and No, where Scrooge's nephew had to think of something, and the rest must find out what; he only answering to their questions yes or no, as the case was. The brisk fire of questioning to which he was exposed, elicited from him that he was thinking of an animal, a live animal, rather a disagreeable animal, a savage animal, an animal that growled and grunted sometimes, and talked sometimes, and lived in London, and walked about the streets, and wasn't made a show of, and wasn't led by anybody, and didn't live in a menagerie, and was never killed in a market, and was not a horse, or an ass, or a cow, or a bull, or a tiger, or a dog, or a pig, or a cat, or a bear. At every fresh question that was put to him, this nephew burst into a fresh roar of laughter;

and was so inexpressibly tickled, that he was obliged to get up off the sofa and stamp. At last the plump sister, falling into a similar state, cried out:

"I have found it out! I know what it is, Fred! I know what it is!"

"What is it?" cried Fred.

"It's your Uncle Scro-o-o-o-oge!"

Which it certainly was. Admiration was the universal sentiment, though some objected that the reply to "Is it a bear?" ought to have been "Yes"; inasmuch as an answer in the negative was sufficient to have diverted their thoughts from Mr. Scrooge, supposing they had ever had any tendency that way.

"He has given us plenty of merriment, I am sure," said Fred, "and it would be ungrateful not to drink his health. Here is a glass of mulled wine ready to our hand at the moment; and I say, 'Uncle Scrooge!' "

"Well! Uncle Scrooge!" they cried.

"A Merry Christmas and a Happy New Year to the old man, whatever he is!" said Scrooge's nephew. "He wouldn't take it from me, but may he have it, nevertheless. Uncle Scrooge!"

Uncle Scrooge had imperceptibly become so gay

and light of heart, that he would have pledged the unconscious company in return, and thanked them in an inaudible speech, if the Ghost had given him time. But the whole scene passed off in the breath of the last word spoken by his nephew; and he and the Spirit were again upon their travels.

Much they saw, and far they went, and many homes they visited, but always with a happy end. The Spirit stood beside sick beds, and they were cheerful; on foreign lands, and they were close at home; by struggling men, and they were patient in their greater hope; by poverty, and it was rich. In almshouse, hospital, and jail, in misery's every refuge, where vain man in his little brief authority had not made fast the door, and barred the Spirit out, he left his blessing, and taught Scrooge his precepts.

It was a long night, if it were only a night; but Scrooge had his doubts of this, because the Christmas Holidays appeared to be condensed into the space of time they passed together. It was strange, too, that while Scrooge remained unaltered in his outward form, the Ghost grew older, clearly older. Scrooge had observed this change, but never spoke of it, until they left a children's Twelfth Night party, when, looking at the Spirit as they stood together in an open place, he noticed that its hair was grey.

"Are spirits' lives so short?" asked Scrooge.

"My life upon this globe, is very brief," replied the Ghost. "It ends to-night."

"To-night!" cried Scrooge.

"To-night at midnight. Hark! The time is drawing near."

The chimes were ringing the three quarters past eleven at that moment.

"Forgive me if I am not justified in what I ask," said Scrooge, looking intently at the Spirit's robe, "but I see something strange, and not belonging to yourself, protruding from your skirts. Is it a foot or a claw?"

"It might be a claw, for the flesh there is upon it," was the Spirit's sorrowful reply. "Look here."

From the foldings of its robe, it brought two children; wretched, abject, frightful, hideous, miserable. They knelt down at its feet, and clung upon the outside of its garment.

"Oh, Man! look here. Look, look, down here!" exclaimed the Ghost.

They were a boy and girl. Yellow, meagre, ragged, scowling, wolfish; but prostrate, too, in their humility. Where graceful youth should have filled their features out, and touched them with its freshest tints, a stale and shrivelled hand, like that of age, had pinched, and twisted them, and pulled them into shreds. Where angels might have sat enthroned, devils lurked, and glared out menacing. No change, no degradation, no perversion of humanity, in any grade, through all the mysteries of wonderful creation, has monsters half so horrible and dread.

Scrooge started back, appalled. Having them shown to him in this way, he tried to say they were fine children, but the words choked themselves, rather than be parties to a lie of such enormous magnitude.

"Spirit! are they yours?" Scrooge could say no more.

"They are Man's," said the Spirit, looking down upon them. "And they cling to me, appealing from their fathers. This boy is Ignorance. This girl is Want. Beware them both, and all of their degree, but most of all beware this boy, for on his brow I see that written which is Doom, unless the writing be erased. Deny it!" cried the Spirit, stretching out its hand towards the city. "Slander those who tell it ye! Admit it for your factious purposes, and make it worse. And bide the end!"

"Have they no refuge or resource?" cried Scrooge.

"Are there no prisons?" said the Spirit, turning on him for the last time with his own words. "Are there no workhouses?"

The bell struck twelve.

Scrooge looked about him for the Ghost, and saw it not. As the last stroke ceased to vibrate, he remembered the prediction of old Jacob Marley, and lifting up his eyes, beheld a solemn Phantom, draped and hooded, coming, like a mist along the ground, towards him.

## Stave Four

# THE LAST OF THE SPIRITS

The Phantom slowly, gravely, silently, approached. When it came near him, Scrooge bent down upon his knee; for in the very air through which this Spirit moved it seemed to scatter gloom and mystery.

It was shrouded in a deep black garment, which concealed its head, its face, its form, and left nothing of it visible save one outstretched hand. But for this it would have been difficult to detach its figure from the night, and separate it from the darkness by which it was surrounded.

He felt that it was tall and stately when it came beside him, and that its mysterious presence filled him with a solemn dread. He knew no more, for the Spirit neither spoke nor moved.

"I am in the presence of the Ghost of Christmas Yet To Come?" said Scrooge.

The Spirit answered not, but pointed onward with its hand.

"You are about to show me shadows of the things that have not happened, but will happen in the time before us," Scrooge pursued. "Is that so, Spirit?"

The upper portion of the garment was contracted for an instant in its folds, as if the Spirit had inclined its head. That was the only answer he received.

Although well used to ghostly company by this

time, Scrooge feared the silent shape so much that his legs trembled beneath him, and he found that he could hardly stand when he prepared to follow it. The Spirit paused a moment, as observing his condition, and giving him time to recover.

But Scrooge was all the worse for this. It thrilled him with a vague uncertain horror, to know that behind the dusky shroud, there were ghostly eyes intently fixed upon him, while he, though he stretched his own to the utmost, could see nothing but a spectral hand and one great heap of black.

"Ghost of the Future!" he exclaimed, "I fear you more than any spectre I have seen. But as I know your purpose is to do me good, and as I hope to live to be another man from what I was, I am prepared to bear you company, and do it with a thankful heart. Will you not speak to me?"

It gave him no reply. The hand was pointed straight before them.

"Lead on!" said Scrooge. "Lead on! The night is waning fast, and it is precious time to me, I know. Lead on, Spirit!"

The Phantom moved away as it had come towards

him. Scrooge followed in the shadow of its dress, which bore him up, he thought, and carried him along.

They scarcely seemed to enter the city; for the city rather seemed to spring up about them, and encompass them of its own act. But there they were, in the heart of it; on 'Change, amongst the merchants; who hurried up and down, and chinked the money in their pockets, and conversed in groups, and looked at their watches, and trifled thoughtfully with their great gold seals; and so forth, as Scrooge had seen them often.

The Spirit stopped beside one little knot of business men. Observing that the hand was pointed to them, Scrooge advanced to listen to their talk.

"No," said a great fat man with a monstrous chin, "I don't know much about it, either way. I only know he's dead."

"When did he die?" inquired another.

"Last night, I believe."

"Why, what was the matter with him?" asked a third, taking a vast quantity of snuff out of a very large snuff-box. "I thought he'd never die."

"God knows," said the first, with a yawn.

"What has he done with his money?" asked a red-faced gentleman with a pendulous excrescence on the end of his nose, that shook like the gills of a turkey-cock.

"I haven't heard," said the man with the large chin, yawning again. "Left it to his company, perhaps. He hasn't left it to *me*. That's all I know."

This pleasantry was received with a general laugh.

"It's likely to be a very cheap funeral," said the same speaker; "for upon my life I don't know of anybody to go to it. Suppose we make up a party and volunteer?"

"I don't mind going if a lunch is provided," observed the gentleman with the excrescence on his nose. "But I must be fed, if I make one."

Another laugh.

"Well, I am the most disinterested among you, after all," said the first speaker, "for I never wear black gloves, and I never eat lunch. But I'll offer to go, if anybody else will. When I come to think of it, I'm not at all sure that I wasn't his most particular friend; for we used to stop and speak whenever we met. Bye, bye!"

Speakers and listeners strolled away, and mixed with other groups. Scrooge knew the men, and looked towards the Spirit for an explanation.

The Phantom glided on into a street. Its finger pointed to two persons meeting. Scrooge listened again, thinking that the explanation might lie here.

He knew these men, also, perfectly. They were men of business: very wealthy, and of great importance. He had made a point always of standing well in their esteem: in a business point of view, that is; strictly in a business point of view.

"How are you?" said one.

"How are you?" returned the other.

"Well!" said the first. "Old Scratch has got his own at last, hey?"

"So I am told," returned the second. "Cold, isn't it?"

"Seasonable for Christmas time. You're not a skater, I suppose?"

"No. No. Something else to think of. Good morning!"

Not another word. That was their meeting, their conversation, and their parting.

Scrooge was at first inclined to be surprised that the Spirit should attach importance to conversations apparently so trivial; but feeling assured that they must have some hidden purpose, he set himself to consider what it was likely to be. They could scarcely be supposed to have any bearing on the death of Jacob, his old partner, for that was Past, and this Ghost's province was the Future. Nor could he think of any one immediately connected with himself, to whom he could apply them. But nothing doubting that to whomsoever they applied they had some latent moral for his own improvement, he resolved to treasure up every word he heard, and everything he saw; and especially to observe the shadow of himself when it appeared. For he had an expectation that the conduct of his future self would give him the clue he missed, and would render the solution of these riddles easy.

He looked about in that very place for his own image; but another man stood in his accustomed corner, and though the clock pointed to his usual time of day for being there, he saw no likeness of himself among the multitudes that poured in through the Porch. It gave him little surprise, however; for he had been revolving in his mind a change of life, and thought and hoped he saw his new-born resolutions carried out in this.

Quiet and dark, beside him stood the Phantom, with its outstretched hand. When he roused himself from his thoughtful quest, he fancied from the turn of the hand, and its situation in reference to himself, that the Unseen Eyes were looking at him keenly. It made him shudder, and feel very cold.

They left the busy scene, and went into an obscure part of the town, where Scrooge had never penetrated before, although he recognised its situation, and its bad repute. The ways were foul and narrow; the shops and houses wretched; the people half-naked, drunken, slipshod, ugly. Alleys and archways, like so many cesspools, disgorged their offences of smell, and dirt, and life, upon the straggling streets; and the whole quarter reeked with crime, with filth, and misery.

Far in this den of infamous resort, there was a low-browed, beetling shop, below a pent-house roof, where iron, old rags, bottles, bones, and greasy offal, were bought. Upon the floor within, were piled up heaps of rusty keys, nails, chains, hinges, files, scales, weights, and refuse iron of all kinds. Secrets that few would like to scrutinise were bred and hidden in mountains of unseemly rags, masses of corrupted fat, and sepulchres of bones. Sitting in among the wares he dealt in, by a charcoal stove, made of old bricks, was a grey-haired rascal, nearly seventy years of age; who had screened himself from the cold air without, by a frousy curtaining of miscellaneous tatters, hung upon a line; and smoked his pipe in all the luxury of calm retirement.

Scrooge and the Phantom came into the presence of this man, just as a woman with a heavy bundle slunk into the shop. But she had scarcely entered, when another woman, similarly laden, came in too; and she was closely followed by a man in faded black, who was no less startled by the sight of them, than they had been upon the recognition of each other. After a short period of blank astonishment, in which the old man with the pipe had joined them, they all three burst into a laugh.

"Let the charwoman alone to be the first!" cried she who had entered first. "Let the laundress alone to be the second; and let the undertaker's man alone to be the third. Look here, old Joe, here's a chance! If we haven't all three met here without meaning it!"

"You couldn't have met in a better place," said old Joe, removing his pipe from his mouth. "Come into the parlour. You were made free of it long ago, you know; and the other two an't strangers. Stop till I shut the door of the shop. Ah! How it skreeks! There an't such a rusty bit of metal in the place as its own hinges, I believe; and I'm sure there's no such old bones here, as mine. Ha, ha! We're all suitable to our calling, we're well matched. Come into the parlour. Come into the parlour."

The parlour was the space behind the screen of rags. The old man raked the fire together with an old stair-rod, and having trimmed his smoky lamp (for it was night), with the stem of his pipe, put it in his mouth again.

While he did this, the woman who had already spoken threw her bundle on the floor, and sat down in a flaunting manner on a stool; crossing her elbows on her knees, and looking with a bold defiance at the other two.

"What odds then! What odds, Mrs. Dilber?" said

the woman. "Every person has a right to take care of themselves. *He* always did."

"That's true, indeed!" said the laundress. "No man more so."

"Why then, don't stand staring as if you was afraid, woman; who's the wiser? We're not going to pick holes in each other's coats, I suppose?"

"No, indeed!" said Mrs. Dilber and the man together. "We should hope not."

"Very well, then!" cried the woman. "That's enough. Who's the worse for the loss of a few things like these? Not a dead man, I suppose."

"No, indeed," said Mrs. Dilber, laughing.

"If he wanted to keep 'em after he was dead, a wicked old screw," pursued the woman, "why wasn't he natural in his lifetime? If he had been, he'd have had somebody to look after him when he was struck with Death, instead of lying gasping out his last there, alone by himself."

"It's the truest word that ever was spoke," said Mrs. Dilber. "It's a judgment on him."

"I wish it was a little heavier judgment," replied the woman; "and it should have been, you may depend upon it, if I could have laid my hands on anything else. Open that bundle, old Joe, and let me know the value of it. Speak out plain. I'm not afraid to be the first, nor afraid for them to see it. We know pretty well that we were helping ourselves, before we met here, I believe. It's no sin. Open the bundle, Joe."

But the gallantry of her friends would not allow of this; and the man in faded black, mounting the breach first, produced *his* plunder. It was not extensive. A seal or two, a pencil-case, a pair of sleeve-buttons, and a brooch of no great value, were all. They were severally examined and appraised by old Joe, who chalked the sums he was disposed to give for each, upon the wall, and added them up into a total when he found there was nothing more to come.

"That's your account," said Joe, "and I wouldn't give another sixpence, if I was to be boiled for not doing it. Who's next?"

Mrs. Dilber was next. Sheets and towels, a little wearing apparel, two old-fashioned silver teaspoons, a pair of sugar-tongs, and a few boots. Her account was stated on the wall in the same manner.

"I always give too much to ladies. It's a weakness of mine, and that's the way I ruin myself," said old Joe. "That's your account. If you asked me for another penny, and made it an open question, I'd repent of being so liberal and knock off half-a-crown."

"And now undo *my* bundle, Joe," said the first woman.

Joe went down on his knees for the greater convenience of opening it, and having unfastened a great many knots, dragged out a large and heavy roll of some dark stuff.

"What do you call this?" said Joe. "Bed-curtains!"

"Ah!" returned the woman, laughing and leaning forward on her crossed arms. "Bed-curtains!"

"You don't mean to say you took 'em down, rings and all, with him lying there?" said Joe.

"Yes I do," replied the woman. "Why not?"

"You were born to make your fortune," said Joe, "and you'll certainly do it."

"I certainly shan't hold my hand, when I can get anything in it by reaching it out, for the sake of such a man as He was, I promise you, Joe," returned the woman coolly. "Don't drop that oil upon the blankets, now."

"His blankets?" asked Joe.

"Whose else's do you think?" replied the woman. "He isn't likely to take cold without 'em, I dare say."

"I hope he didn't die of anything catching? Eh?" said old Joe, stopping in his work, and looking up.

"Don't you be afraid of that," returned the woman. "I an't so fond of his company that I'd loiter about him for such things, if he did. Ah! you may look through that shirt till your eyes ache; but you won't find a hole in it, nor a threadbare place. It's the best he had, and a fine one too. They'd have wasted it, if it hadn't been for me."

"What do you call wasting of it?" asked old Joe.

"Putting it on him to be buried in, to be sure," replied the woman with a laugh. "Somebody was fool enough to do it, but I took it off again. If calico an't good enough for such a purpose, it isn't good enough for anything. It's quite as becoming to the body. He can't look uglier than he did in that one."

Scrooge listened to this dialogue in horror. As they sat grouped about their spoil, in the scanty light afforded by the old man's lamp, he viewed them with a detestation and disgust, which could hardly have been greater, though they had been obscene demons, marketing the corpse itself.

"Ha, ha!" laughed the same woman, when old Joe, producing a flannel bag with money in it, told out their several gains upon the ground. "This is the end of it, you see! He frightened every one away from him when he was alive, to profit us when he was dead! Ha, ha, ha!"

"Spirit!" said Scrooge, shuddering from head to foot. "I see, I see. The case of this unhappy man might be my own. My life tends that way, now. Merciful Heaven, what is this!"

He recoiled in terror, for the scene had changed, and now he almost touched a bed: a bare, uncurtained bed: on which, beneath a ragged sheet, there lay a something covered up, which, though it was dumb, announced itself in awful language.

The room was very dark, too dark to be observed with any accuracy, though Scrooge glanced round it in obedience to a secret impulse, anxious to know what kind of room it was. A pale light, rising in the outer air, fell straight upon the bed; and on it, plundered and bereft, unwatched, unwept, uncared for, was the body of this man.

Scrooge glanced towards the Phantom. Its steady hand was pointed to the head. The cover was so carelessly adjusted that the slightest raising of it, the motion of a finger upon Scrooge's part, would have disclosed the face. He thought of it, felt how easy it would be to do, and longed to do it; but had no more power to withdraw the veil than to dismiss the spectre at his side.

Oh cold, cold, rigid, dreadful Death, set up thine altar here, and dress it with such terrors as thou hast at thy command: for this is thy dominion! But of the loved, revered, and honoured head, thou canst not turn one hair to thy dread purposes, or make one feature odious. It is not that the hand is heavy and will fall down when released; it is not that the heart and pulse are still; but that the hand *was* open, generous, and true; the heart brave, warm, and tender; and the pulse a man's. Strike, Shadow, strike! And see his good deeds springing from the wound, to sow the world with life immortal!

No voice pronounced these words in Scrooge's ears, and yet he heard them when he looked upon the bed. He thought, if this man could be raised up now, what would be his foremost thoughts? Avarice, hard-dealing, griping cares? They have brought him to a rich end, truly!

He lay, in the dark empty house, with not a man, a woman, or a child, to say that he was kind to me in this or that, and for the memory of one kind word I will be kind to him. A cat was tearing at the door, and there was a sound of gnawing rats beneath the hearth-stone. What *they* wanted in the room of death, and why they were so restless and disturbed, Scrooge did not dare to think.

"Spirit!" he said, "this is a fearful place. In leaving it, I shall not leave its lesson, trust me. Let us go!"

Still the Ghost pointed with an unmoved finger to the head.

"I understand you," Scrooge returned, "and I would do it, if I could. But I have not the power, Spirit. I have not the power."

Again it seemed to look upon him.

"If there is any person in the town, who feels

emotion caused by this man's death," said Scrooge quite agonised, "show that person to me, Spirit, I beseech you!"

The Phantom spread its dark robe before him for a moment, like a wing; and withdrawing it, revealed a room by daylight, where a mother and her children were.

She was expecting some one, and with anxious eagerness; for she walked up and down the room; started at every sound; looked out from the window; glanced at the clock; tried, but in vain, to work with her needle; and could hardly bear the voices of the children in their play.

At length the long-expected knock was heard. She hurried to the door, and met her husband; a man whose face was careworn and depressed, though he was young. There was a remarkable expression in it now; a kind of serious delight of which he felt ashamed, and which he struggled to repress.

He sat down to the dinner that had been hoarding for him by the fire; and when she asked him faintly what news (which was not until after a long silence), he appeared embarrassed how to answer.

"Is it good?" she said, "or bad?"—to help him.

"Bad," he answered.

"We are quite ruined?"

"No. There is hope yet, Caroline."

"If *he* relents," she said, amazed, "there is! Nothing is past hope, if such a miracle has happened."

"He is past relenting," said her husband. "He is dead."

She was a mild and patient creature if her face spoke truth; but she was thankful in her soul to hear it, and she said so, with clasped hands. She prayed forgiveness the next moment, and was sorry; but the first was the emotion of her heart.

"What the half-drunken woman whom I told you of last night, said to me, when I tried to see him and obtain a week's delay; and what I thought was a mere excuse to avoid me; turns out to have been quite true. He was not only very ill, but dying, then."

"To whom will our debt be transferred?"

"I don't know. But before that time we shall be ready with the money; and even though we were not, it would be a bad fortune indeed to find so merciless a creditor in his successor. We may sleep to-night with light hearts, Caroline!"

Yes. Soften it as they would, their hearts were lighter. The children's faces, hushed and clustered round to hear what they so little understood, were brighter; and it was a happier house for this man's death! The only emotion that the Ghost could show him, caused by the event, was one of pleasure.

"Let me see some tenderness connected with a death," said Scrooge; "or that dark chamber, Spirit, which we left just now, will be for ever present to me."

The Ghost conducted him through several streets familiar to his feet; and as they went along, Scrooge looked here and there to find himself, but nowhere was he to be seen. They entered poor Bob Cratchit's house; the dwelling he had visited before; and found the mother and the children seated round the fire.

Quiet. Very quiet. The noisy little Cratchits were as still as statues in one corner, and sat looking up at Peter, who had a book before him. The mother and her daughters were engaged in sewing. But surely they were very quiet!

"'And He took a child, and set him in the midst of them.'"

Where had Scrooge heard those words? He had not dreamed them. The boy must have read them out, as he and the Spirit crossed the threshold. Why did he not go on?

The mother laid her work upon the table, and put her hand up to her face.

"The colour hurts my eyes," she said.

The colour? Ah, poor Tiny Tim!

"They're better now again," said Cratchit's wife. "It makes them weak by candle-light; and I wouldn't show weak eyes to your father when he comes home, for the world. It must be near his time."

"Past it rather," Peter answered, shutting up his book. "But I think he has walked a little slower than he used, these few last evenings, mother."

They were very quiet again. At last she said, and in a steady, cheerful voice, that only faltered once:

"I have known him walk with—I have known him walk with Tiny Tim upon his shoulder, very fast indeed."

"And so have I," cried Peter. "Often."

"And so have I," exclaimed another. So had all.

"But he was very light to carry," she resumed, intent upon her work, "and his father loved him so, that it was no trouble: no trouble. And there is your father at the door!"

She hurried out to meet him; and little Bob in his comforter—he had need of it, poor fellow—came in. His tea was ready for him on the hob, and they all tried who should help him to it most. Then the two young Cratchits got upon his knees and laid, each child a little cheek, against his face, as if they said, "Don't mind it, father. Don't be grieved!"

Bob was very cheerful with them, and spoke pleasantly to all the family. He looked at the work upon the table, and praised the industry and speed of Mrs. Cratchit and the girls. They would be done long before Sunday, he said.

"Sunday! You went to-day, then, Robert?" said his wife.

"Yes, my dear," returned Bob. "I wish you could have gone. It would have done you good to see how green a place it is. But you'll see it often. I promised him that I would walk there on a Sunday. My little, little child!" cried Bob. "My little child!"

He broke down all at once. He couldn't help it. If he could have helped it, he and his child would have been farther apart perhaps than they were.

He left the room, and went up-stairs into the room above, which was lighted cheerfully, and hung with Christmas. There was a chair set close beside the child, and there were signs of some one having been there, lately. Poor Bob sat down in it, and when he had thought a little and composed himself, he kissed the little face. He was reconciled to what had happened, and went down again quite happy.

They drew about the fire, and talked; the girls and mother working still. Bob told them of the extraordinary kindness of Mr. Scrooge's nephew, whom he had scarcely seen but once, and who, meeting him in the street that day, and seeing that he looked a little—"Just a little down you know," said Bob, inquired what had happened to distress him. "On which," said Bob, "for he is the pleasantest-spoken gentleman you ever heard, I told him. 'I am heartily sorry for it, Mr. Cratchit,' he said, 'and heartily sorry for your good wife.' By the bye, how he ever knew *that*, I don't know."

"Knew what, my dear?"

"Why, that you were a good wife," replied Bob.

"Everybody knows that!" said Peter.

"Very well observed, my boy!" cried Bob. "I hope they do. 'Heartily sorry,' he said, 'for your good wife. If I can be of service to you in any way,' he said, giving me his card, 'that's where I live. Pray come to me.' Now, it wasn't," cried Bob, "for the sake of anything he might be able to do for us, so much as for his kind way, that this was quite delightful. It really seemed as if he had known our Tiny Tim, and felt with us."

"I'm sure he's a good soul!" said Mrs. Cratchit.

"You would be surer of it, my dear," returned Bob, "if you saw and spoke to him. I shouldn't be at all surprised—mark what I say!—if he got Peter a better situation."

"Only hear that, Peter," said Mrs. Cratchit.

"And then," cried one of the girls, "Peter will be keeping company with some one, and setting up for himself."

"Get along with you!" retorted Peter, grinning.

"It's just as likely as not," said Bob, "one of these days; though there's plenty of time for that, my dear. But however and whenever we part from one another, I am sure we shall none of us forget poor Tiny Tim—shall we—or this first parting that there was among us?"

"Never, father!" cried they all.

"And I know," said Bob, "I know, my dears, that when we recollect how patient and how mild he was; although he was a little, little child; we shall not quarrel easily among ourselves, and forget poor Tiny Tim in doing it."

"No, never, father!" they all cried again.

"I am very happy," said little Bob, "I am very happy!"

Mrs. Cratchit kissed him, his daughters kissed him, the two young Cratchits kissed him, and Peter and himself shook hands. Spirit of Tiny Tim, thy childish essence was from God!

"Spectre," said Scrooge, "something informs me that our parting moment is at hand. I know it, but I know not how. Tell me what man that was whom we saw lying dead?"

The Ghost of Christmas Yet To Come conveyed him, as before—though at a different time, he thought:

indeed, there seemed no order in these latter visions, save that they were in the Future—into the resorts of business men, but showed him not himself. Indeed, the Spirit did not stay for anything, but went straight on, as to the end just now desired, until besought by Scrooge to tarry for a moment.

"This court," said Scrooge, "through which we hurry now, is where my place of occupation is, and has been for a length of time. I see the house. Let me behold what I shall be, in days to come!"

The Spirit stopped; the hand was pointed elsewhere.

"The house is yonder," Scrooge exclaimed. "Why do you point away?"

The inexorable finger underwent no change.

Scrooge hastened to the window of his office, and looked in. It was an office still, but not his. The furniture was not the same, and the figure in the chair was not himself. The Phantom pointed as before.

He joined it once again, and wondering why and whither he had gone, accompanied it until they reached an iron gate. He paused to look round before entering.

A churchyard. Here, then; the wretched man

whose name he had now to learn, lay underneath the ground. It was a worthy place. Walled in by houses; overrun by grass and weeds, the growth of vegetation's death, not life; choked up with too much burying; fat with repleted appetite. A worthy place!

The Spirit stood among the graves, and pointed down to One. He advanced towards it trembling. The Phantom was exactly as it had been, but he dreaded that he saw new meaning in its solemn shape.

"Before I draw nearer to that stone to which you point," said Scrooge, "answer me one question. Are these the shadows of the things that Will be, or are they shadows of things that May be, only?"

Still the Ghost pointed downward to the grave by which it stood.

"Men's courses will foreshadow certain ends, to which, if persevered in, they must lead," said Scrooge. "But if the courses be departed from, the ends will change. Say it is thus with what you show me!"

The Spirit was immovable as ever.

Scrooge crept towards it, trembling as he went; and following the finger, read upon the stone of the neglected grave his own name, EBENEZER SCROOGE.

"Am *I* that man who lay upon the bed?" he cried, upon his knees.

The finger pointed from the grave to him, and back again.

"No, Spirit! Oh no, no!"

The finger still was there.

"Spirit!" he cried, tight clutching at its robe, "hear me! I am not the man I was. I will not be the man I must have been but for this intercourse. Why show me this, if I am past all hope!"

For the first time the hand appeared to shake.

"Good Spirit," he pursued, as down upon the ground he fell before it: "Your nature intercedes for me, and pities me. Assure me that I yet may change these shadows you have shown me, by an altered life!"

The kind hand trembled.

"I will honour Christmas in my heart, and try to keep it all the year. I will live in the Past, the Present, and the Future. The Spirits of all Three shall strive within me. I will not shut out the lessons that they teach. Oh, tell me I may sponge away the writing on this stone!"

In his agony, he caught the spectral hand. It sought to free itself, but he was strong in his entreaty, and detained it. The Spirit, stronger yet, repulsed him.

Holding up his hands in a last prayer to have his fate reversed, he saw an alteration in the Phantom's hood and dress. It shrunk, collapsed, and dwindled down into a bedpost.

## Stave Five

# THE END OF IT

Yes! and the bedpost was his own. The bed was his own, the room was his own. Best and happiest of all, the Time before him was his own, to make amends in!

"I will live in the Past, the Present, and the Future!" Scrooge repeated, as he scrambled out of bed. "The Spirits of all Three shall strive within me. Oh Jacob Marley! Heaven, and the Christmas Time be praised for this! I say it on my knees, old Jacob; on my knees!"

He was so fluttered and so glowing with his good intentions, that his broken voice would scarcely answer to his call. He had been sobbing violently in his conflict with the Spirit, and his face was wet with tears.

"They are not torn down," cried Scrooge, folding one of his bed-curtains in his arms, "they are not torn down, rings and all. They are here—I am here—the shadows of the things that would have been, may be dispelled. They will be. I know they will!"

His hands were busy with his garments all this time; turning them inside out, putting them on upside down, tearing them, mislaying them, making them parties to every kind of extravagance.

"I don't know what to do!" cried Scrooge, laughing and crying in the same breath; and making a perfect Laocoön of himself with his stockings. "I am as light as a feather, I am as happy as an angel, I am as merry as a schoolboy. I am as giddy as a drunken man. A merry Christmas to everybody! A happy New Year to all the world. Hallo here! Whoop! Hallo!"

He had frisked into the sitting-room, and was now standing there: perfectly winded.

"There's the saucepan that the gruel was in!"

cried Scrooge, starting off again, and going round the fireplace. "There's the door, by which the Ghost of Jacob Marley entered! There's the corner where the Ghost of Christmas Present sat! There's the window where I saw the wandering Spirits! It's all right, it's all true, it all happened. Ha ha ha!"

Really, for a man who had been out of practice for so many years, it was a splendid laugh, a most illustrious laugh. The father of a long, long line of brilliant laughs!

"I don't know what day of the month it is!" said Scrooge. "I don't know how long I've been among the Spirits. I don't know anything. I'm quite a baby. Never mind. I don't care. I'd rather be a baby. Hallo! Whoop! Hallo here!"

He was checked in his transports by the churches ringing out the lustiest peals he had ever heard. Clash, clang, hammer; ding, dong, bell. Bell, dong, ding; hammer, clang, clash! Oh, glorious, glorious!

Running to the window, he opened it, and put out his head. No fog, no mist; clear, bright, jovial, stirring, cold; cold, piping for the blood to dance to; Golden sunlight; Heavenly sky; sweet fresh air; merry bells. Oh, glorious! Glorious!

"What's to-day!" cried Scrooge, calling downward to a boy in Sunday clothes, who perhaps had loitered in to look about him.

"*Eh?*" returned the boy, with all his might of wonder.

"What's to-day, my fine fellow?" said Scrooge.

"To-day!" replied the boy. "Why, CHRISTMAS DAY."

"It's Christmas Day!" said Scrooge to himself. "I haven't missed it. The Spirits have done it all in one night. They can do anything they like. Of course they can. Of course they can. Hallo, my fine fellow!"

"Hallo!" returned the boy.

"Do you know the Poulterer's, in the next street but one, at the corner?" Scrooge inquired.

"I should hope I did," replied the lad.

"An intelligent boy!" said Scrooge. "A remarkable boy! Do you know whether they've sold the prize Turkey that was hanging up there?—Not the little prize Turkey: the big one?"

"What, the one as big as me?" returned the boy.

"What a delightful boy!" said Scrooge. "It's a pleasure to talk to him. Yes, my buck!"

"It's hanging there now," replied the boy.

"Is it?" said Scrooge. "Go and buy it."

"Walk-ER!" exclaimed the boy.

"No, no," said Scrooge, "I am in earnest. Go and buy it, and tell 'em to bring it here, that I may give them the direction where to take it. Come back with the man, and I'll give you a shilling. Come back with him in less than five minutes and I'll give you half-a-crown!"

The boy was off like a shot. He must have had a steady hand at a trigger who could have got a shot off half so fast.

"I'll send it to Bob Cratchit's!" whispered Scrooge, rubbing his hands, and splitting with a laugh. "He sha'n't know who sends it. It's twice the size of Tiny Tim. Joe Miller never made such a joke as sending it to Bob's will be!"

The hand in which he wrote the address was not a steady one, but write it he did, somehow, and went down-stairs to open the street door, ready for the coming of the poulterer's man. As he stood there, waiting his arrival, the knocker caught his eye.

"I shall love it, as long as I live!" cried Scrooge, patting it with his hand. "I scarcely ever looked at it before. What an honest expression it has in its face! It's a wonderful knocker!—Here's the Turkey! Hallo! Whoop! How are you! Merry Christmas!"

It *was* a Turkey! He never could have stood upon his legs, that bird. He would have snapped 'em short off in a minute, like sticks of sealing-wax.

"Why, it's impossible to carry that to Camden Town," said Scrooge. "You must have a cab."

The chuckle with which he said this, and the chuckle with which he paid for the Turkey, and the chuckle with which he paid for the cab, and the chuckle with which he recompensed the boy, were only to be exceeded by the chuckle with which he sat down breathless in his chair again, and chuckled till he cried.

Shaving was not an easy task, for his hand continued to shake very much; and shaving requires attention, even when you don't dance while you are at it. But if he had cut the end of his nose off, he would have put a piece of sticking-plaister over it, and been quite satisfied.

He dressed himself "all in his best," and at last

got out into the streets. The people were by this time pouring forth, as he had seen them with the Ghost of Christmas Present; and walking with his hands behind him, Scrooge regarded every one with a delighted smile. He looked so irresistibly pleasant, in a word, that three or four good-humoured fellows said, "Good morning, sir! A merry Christmas to you!" And Scrooge said often afterwards, that of all the blithe sounds he had ever heard, those were the blithest in his ears.

He had not gone far, when coming on towards him he beheld the portly gentleman, who had walked into his counting-house the day before, and said, "Scrooge and Marley's, I believe?" It sent a pang across his heart to think how this old gentleman would look upon him when they met; but he knew what path lay straight before him, and he took it.

"My dear sir," said Scrooge, quickening his pace, and taking the old gentleman by both his hands. "How do you do? I hope you succeeded yesterday. It was very kind of you. A merry Christmas to you, sir!"

"Mr. Scrooge?"

"Yes," said Scrooge. "That is my name, and I fear

it may not be pleasant to you. Allow me to ask your pardon. And will you have the goodness"—here Scrooge whispered in his ear.

"Lord bless me!" cried the gentleman, as if his breath were taken away. "My dear Mr. Scrooge, are you serious?"

"If you please," said Scrooge. "Not a farthing less. A great many back-payments are included in it, I assure you. Will you do me that favour?"

"My dear sir," said the other, shaking hands with him. "I don't know what to say to such munifi—"

"Don't say anything, please," retorted Scrooge. "Come and see me. Will you come and see me?"

"I will!" cried the old gentleman. And it was clear he meant to do it.

"Thank'ee," said Scrooge. "I am much obliged to you. I thank you fifty times. Bless you!"

He went to church, and walked about the streets, and watched the people hurrying to and fro, and patted children on the head, and questioned beggars, and looked down into the kitchens of houses, and up to the windows, and found that everything could yield him pleasure. He had never dreamed that any walk—that anything—could give him so much happiness. In the afternoon he turned his steps towards his nephew's house.

He passed the door a dozen times, before he had the courage to go up and knock. But he made a dash, and did it:

"Is your master at home, my dear?" said Scrooge to the girl. Nice girl! Very.

"Yes, sir."

"Where is he, my love?" said Scrooge.

"He's in the dining-room, sir, along with mistress. I'll show you up-stairs, if you please."

"Thank'ee. He knows me," said Scrooge, with his hand already on the dining-room lock. "I'll go in here, my dear."

He turned it gently, and sidled his face in, round the door. They were looking at the table (which was spread out in great array); for these young housekeepers are always nervous on such points, and like to see that everything is right.

"Fred!" said Scrooge.

Dear heart alive, how his niece by marriage started! Scrooge had forgotten, for the moment, about her sitting in the corner with the footstool, or he wouldn't have done it, on any account.

"Why bless my soul!" cried Fred, "who's that?"

"It's I. Your uncle Scrooge. I have come to dinner. Will you let me in, Fred?"

Let him in! It is a mercy he didn't shake his arm off. He was at home in five minutes. Nothing could be heartier. His niece looked just the same. So did Topper when *he* came. So did the plump sister when *she* came. So did every one when *they* came. Wonderful party, wonderful games, wonderful unanimity, won-der-ful happiness!

But he was early at the office next morning. Oh, he was early there. If he could only be there first, and catch Bob Cratchit coming late! That was the thing he had set his heart upon.

And he did it; yes, he did! The clock struck nine. No Bob. A quarter past. No Bob. He was full eighteen minutes and a half behind his time. Scrooge sat with his door wide open, that he might see him come into the Tank.

His hat was off before he opened the door; his comforter too. He was on his stool in a jiffy; driving away with his pen, as if he were trying to overtake nine o'clock.

"Hallo!" growled Scrooge, in his accustomed voice, as near as he could feign it. "What do you mean by coming here at this time of day?"

"I am very sorry, sir," said Bob. "I *am* behind my time."

"You are?" repeated Scrooge. "Yes. I think you are. Step this way, sir, if you please."

"It's only once a year, sir," pleaded Bob, appearing from the Tank. "It shall not be repeated. I was making rather merry yesterday, sir."

"Now, I'll tell you what, my friend," said Scrooge, "I am not going to stand this sort of thing any longer. And therefore," he continued, leaping from his stool, and giving Bob such a dig in the waistcoat that he staggered back into the Tank again; "and therefore I am about to raise your salary!"

Bob trembled, and got a little nearer to the ruler. He had a momentary idea of knocking Scrooge down with it, holding him, and calling to the people in the court for help and a strait-waistcoat.

"A merry Christmas, Bob!" said Scrooge, with an earnestness that could not be mistaken, as he clapped him on the back. "A merrier Christmas, Bob, my good fellow, than I have given you, for many a year! I'll raise your salary, and endeavour to assist your struggling family, and we will discuss your affairs this very afternoon, over a Christmas bowl of smoking bishop, Bob! Make up the fires, and buy another coal-scuttle before you dot another *i*, Bob Cratchit!"

Scrooge was better than his word. He did it all, and infinitely more; and to Tiny Tim, who did *not* die, he was a second father. He became as good a friend, as good a master, and as good a man, as the good old city knew, or any other good old city, town, or borough, in the good old world. Some people laughed to see the alteration in him, but he let them laugh, and little heeded them; for he was wise enough to know that nothing ever happened on this globe, for good, at which some people did not have their fill of laughter in the outset; and knowing that such as these would be blind anyway, he thought it quite as well that they should wrinkle up their eyes in grins, as have the malady in less attractive forms. His own heart laughed: and that was quite enough for him.

He had no further intercourse with Spirits, but lived upon the Total Abstinence Principle, ever afterwards; and it was always said of him, that he knew how to keep Christmas well, if any man alive possessed the knowledge. May that be truly said of us, and all of us! And so, as Tiny Tim observed, God bless Us, Every One!

# LOUISA MAY ALCOTT

1832–1888

# TILLY'S CHRISTMAS

"I'm so glad to-morrow is Christmas, because I'm going to have lots of presents."

"So am I glad, though I don't expect any presents but a pair of mittens."

"And so am I; but I shan't have any presents at all."

As the three little girls trudged home from school, they said these things, and as Tilly spoke, both the others looked at her with pity and some surprise, for she spoke cheerfully, and they wondered how she could be happy when she was so poor she could have no presents on Christmas.

"Don't you wish you could find a purse full of money right here in the path?" said Kate, the child who was going to have "lots of presents."

"Oh, don't I, if I could keep it honestly!" and Tilly's eyes shone at the very thought.

"What would you buy?" asked Bessy, rubbing her cold hands, and longing for her mittens.

"I'd buy a pair of large, warm blankets, a load of wood, a shawl for mother, and a pair of shoes for me; and if there was enough left, I'd give Bessy a new hat, and then she needn't wear Ben's old felt one," answered Tilly.

The girls laughed at that; but Bessy pulled the funny hat over her ears, and said she was much obliged but she'd rather have candy.

"Let's look, and maybe we *can* find a purse. People are always going about with money at Christmas time, and some one may lose it here," said Kate.

So, as they went along the snowy road, they looked about them, half in earnest, half in fun. Suddenly Tilly sprang forward, exclaiming—

"I see it! I've found it!"

The others followed, but all stopped disappointed;

for it wasn't a purse, it was only a little bird. It lay upon the snow with its wings spread and feebly fluttering, as if too weak to fly. Its little feet were benumbed with cold; its once bright eyes were dull with pain, and instead of a blithe song, it could only utter a faint chirp now and then, as if crying for help.

"Nothing but a stupid old robin; how provoking!" cried Kate, sitting down to rest.

"I shan't touch it. I found one once, and took care of it, and the ungrateful thing flew away the minute it was well," said Bessy, creeping under Kate's shawl, and putting her hands under her chin to warm them.

"Poor little birdie! How pitiful he looks, and how glad he must be to see some one coming to help him! I'll take him up gently, and carry him home to mother. Don't be frightened, dear, I'm your friend"; and Tilly knelt down in the snow, stretching her hand to the bird, with the tenderest pity in her face.

Kate and Bessy laughed.

"Don't stop for that thing; it's getting late and cold: let's go on and look for the purse," they said, moving away.

"You wouldn't leave it to die!" cried Tilly. "I'd

rather have the bird than the money, so I shan't look any more. The purse wouldn't be mine, and I should only be tempted to keep it; but this poor thing will thank and love me, and I'm *so* glad I came in time."

Gently lifting the bird, Tilly felt its tiny cold claws cling to her hand, and saw its dim eyes brighten as it nestled down with a grateful chirp.

"Now I've got a Christmas present after all," she said, smiling, as they walked on. "I always wanted a bird, and this one will be such a pretty pet for me."

"He'll fly away the first chance he gets, and die anyhow; so you'd better not waste your time over him," said Bessy.

"He can't pay you for taking care of him, and my mother says it isn't worth while to help folks that can't help us," added Kate.

"My mother says, 'Do as you'd be done by'; and I'm sure I'd like any one to help me if I was dying of cold and hunger. 'Love your neighbour as yourself,' is another of her sayings. This bird is my little neighbour, and I'll love him and care for him, as I often wish our rich neighbour would love and care for us," answered Tilly, breathing her warm breath over the benumbed bird, who looked up at her with confiding eyes, quick to feel and know a friend.

"What a funny girl you are," said Kate; "caring for that silly bird, and talking about loving your neighbour in that sober way. Mr. King don't care a bit for you, and never will, though he knows how poor you are; so I don't think your plan amounts to much."

"I believe it, though; and shall do my part, any way. Good-night. I hope you'll have a merry Christmas, and lots of pretty things," answered Tilly as they parted.

Her eyes were full, and she felt so poor as she went on alone toward the little old house where she lived. It would have been so pleasant to know that she was going to have some of the pretty things all children love to find in their full stockings on Christmas morning. And pleasanter still to have been able to give her mother something nice. So many comforts were needed, and there was no hope of getting them; for they could barely get food and fire.

"Never mind, birdie, we'll make the best of what we have, and be merry in spite of every thing. *You* shall have a happy Christmas any way; and I know God won't forget us if every one else does."

She stopped a minute to wipe her eyes and lean her cheek against the bird's soft breast, finding great comfort in the little creature, though it could only love her, nothing more.

"See, mother, what a nice present I've found," she cried, going in with a cheery face that was like sunshine in the dark room.

"I'm glad of that, dearie; for I haven't been able to get my little girl anything but a rosy apple. Poor bird! Give it some of your warm bread and milk."

"Why, mother, what a big bowlful! I'm afraid you gave me all the milk," said Tilly, smiling over the nice, steaming supper that stood ready for her.

"I've had plenty, dear. Sit down and dry your wet feet, and put the bird in my basket on this warm flannel."

Tilly peeped into the closet and saw nothing there but dry bread.

"Mother's given me all the milk, and is going without her tea, 'cause she knows I'm hungry. Now I'll surprise her, and she shall have a good supper too. She is going to split wood, and I'll fix it while she's gone."

So Tilly put down the old tea-pot, carefully poured out a part of the milk, and from her pocket produced a great, plummy bun that one of the school-children had given her and she had saved for her mother. A slice of the dry bread was nicely toasted, and the bit of butter set by for her put on it. When her mother came in, there was the table drawn up in a warm place, a hot cup of tea ready, and Tilly and birdie waiting for her.

Such a poor little supper, and yet such a happy one; for love, charity, and contentment were guests there, and that Christmas eve was a blither one than that up at the great house, where lights shone, fires blazed, a great tree glittered, and music sounded, as the children danced and played.

"We must go to bed early, for we've only wood enough to last over to-morrow. I shall be paid for my work the day after, and then we can get some," said Tilly's mother, as they sat by the fire.

"If my bird was only a fairy bird, and would give us three wishes, how nice it would be! Poor dear, he can't give me any thing; but it's no matter," answered Tilly, looking at the robin, who lay in the basket

165

with his head under his wing, a mere little feathery bunch.

"He can give you one thing, Tilly—the pleasure of doing good. That is one of the sweetest things in life; and the poor can enjoy it as well as the rich."

As her mother spoke, with her tired hand softly stroking her little daughter's hair, Tilly suddenly started and pointed to the window, saying, in a frightened whisper—

"I saw a face—a man's face, looking in! It's gone now; but I truly saw it."

"Some traveller attracted by the light perhaps. I'll go and see." And Tilly's mother went to the door.

No one was there. The wind blew cold, the stars shone, the snow lay white on field and wood, and the Christmas moon was glittering in the sky.

"What sort of a face was it?" asked Tilly's mother, coming back.

"A pleasant sort of face, I think; but I was so startled I don't quite know what it was like. I wish we had a curtain there," said Tilly.

"I like to have our light shine out in the evening, for the road is dark and lonely just here, and the twinkle of our lamp is pleasant to people's eyes as they go by. We can do so little for our neighbours, I am glad to cheer the way for them. Now put these poor old shoes to dry, and go to bed, dearie; I'll come soon."

Tilly went, taking her bird with her to sleep in his basket near by, lest he should be lonely in the night.

Soon the little house was dark and still, and no one saw the Christmas spirits at their work that night.

When Tilly opened the door next morning, she gave a loud cry, clapped her hands, and then stood still; quite speechless with wonder and delight. There, before the door, lay a great pile of wood, all ready to burn, a big bundle and a basket, with a lovely nosegay of winter roses, holly, and evergreen tied to the handle.

"Oh, mother! did the fairies do it?" cried Tilly, pale with her happiness, as she seized the basket, while her mother took in the bundle.

"Yes, dear, the best and dearest fairy in the world, called 'Charity.' She walks abroad at Christmas time, does beautiful deeds like this, and does not stay to be thanked," answered her mother with full eyes, as she undid the parcel.

There they were—the warm, thick blankets, the comfortable shawls, the new shoes, and, best of all, a pretty winter hat for Bessy. The basket was full of good things to eat, and on the flowers lay a paper, saying—

"For the little girl who loves her neighbour as herself."

"Mother, I really think my bird is a fairy bird, and all these splendid things come from him," said Tilly, laughing and crying with joy.

It really did seem so, for as she spoke, the robin flew to the table, hopped to the nosegay, and perching among the roses, began to chirp with all his little might. The sun streamed in on flowers, bird, and happy child, and no one saw a shadow glide away from the window; no one ever knew that Mr. King had seen and heard the little girls the night before, or dreamed that the rich neighbour had learned a lesson from the poor neighbour.

And Tilly's bird *was* a fairy bird; for by her love and tenderness to the helpless thing, she brought good gifts to herself, happiness to the unknown giver of them, and a faithful little friend who did not fly away, but stayed with her till the snow was gone, making summer for her in the winter-time.

# TESSA'S SURPRISES

## I.

Little Tessa sat alone by the fire, waiting for her father to come home from work. The children were fast asleep, all four in the big bed behind the curtain; the wind blew hard outside, and the snow beat on the window-panes; the room was large, and the fire so small and feeble that it didn't half warm the little bare toes peeping out of the old shoes on the hearth.

Tessa's father was an Italian plaster-worker, very poor, but kind and honest. The mother had died not long ago, and left twelve-year-old Tessa to take care of the little children. She tried to be very wise and motherly, and worked for them like any little woman; but it was so hard to keep the small bodies warm and fed, and the small souls good and happy, that poor Tessa was often at her wits' end. She always waited for her father, no matter how tired she was, so that he might find his supper warm, a bit of fire, and a loving little face to welcome him. Tessa thought over her troubles at these quiet times, and made her plans; for her father left things to her a good deal, and she had no friends but Tommo, the harp-boy upstairs, and the lively cricket who lived in the chimney. To-night her face was very sober, and her pretty brown eyes very thoughtful as she stared at the fire and knit her brows, as if perplexed. She was not thinking of her old shoes, nor the empty closet, nor the boys' ragged clothes just then. No; she had a fine plan in her good little head, and was trying to discover how she could carry it out.

You see, Christmas was coming in a week; and she had set her heart on putting something in the children's stockings, as the mother used to do, for while she lived things were comfortable. Now Tessa had not a penny in the world, and didn't know how to get one, for all the father's earnings had to go for food, fire, and rent.

"If there were only fairies, ah! how heavenly that would be; for then I should tell them all I wish, and, pop! behold the fine things in my lap!" said Tessa to herself. "I must earn the money; there is no one to give it to me, and I cannot beg. But what can I do, so small and stupid and shy as I am? I *must* find some way to give the little ones a nice Christmas. I *must*! I *must*!" and Tessa pulled her long hair, as if that would help her think.

But it didn't, and her heart got heavier and heavier; for it did seem hard that in a great city full of fine things, there should be none for poor Nono, Sep, and little Speranza. Just as Tessa's tears began to tumble off her eyelashes on to her brown cheeks, the cricket began to chirp. Of course, he didn't say a word; but it really did seem as if he had answered her question almost as well as a fairy; for, before he had piped a dozen shrill notes, an idea popped into Tessa's head—such a truly splendid idea that she clapped her hands and burst out laughing. "I'll do it! I'll do it! if father will let me," she said to herself, smiling and nodding at the fire. "Tommo will like to have me go with him and sing, while he plays his harp in the streets. I know many songs, and may get money if I am not frightened; for people throw pennies to other little girls who only play the tambourine. Yes, I will try; and then, if I do well, the little ones shall have a Merry Christmas."

So full of her plan was Tessa that she ran upstairs at once, and asked Tommo if he would take her with him on the morrow. Her friend was delighted, for he thought Tessa's songs very sweet, and was sure she would get money if she tried.

"But see, then, it is cold in the streets; the wind bites, and the snow freezes one's fingers. The day is very long, people are cross, and at night one is ready to die with weariness. Thou art so small, Tessa, I am afraid it will go badly with thee," said Tommo, who was a merry, black-eyed boy of fourteen, with the kindest heart in the world under his old jacket.

"I do not mind cold and wet, and cross people, if I can get the pennies," answered Tessa, feeling very brave with such a friend to help her. She thanked

Tommo, and ran away to get ready, for she felt sure her father would not refuse her anything. She sewed up the holes in her shoes as well as she could, for she had much of that sort of cobbling to do; she mended her only gown, and laid ready the old hood and shawl which had been her mother's. Then she washed out little Ranza's frock and put it to dry, because she would not be able to do it the next day. She set the table and got things ready for breakfast, for Tommo went out early, and must not be kept waiting for her. She longed to make the beds and dress the children over night, she was in such a hurry to have all in order; but, as that could not be, she sat down again, and tried over all the songs she knew. Six pretty ones were chosen; and she sang away with all her heart in a fresh little voice so sweetly that the children smiled in their sleep, and her father's tired face brightened as he entered, for Tessa was his cheery cricket on the hearth. When she had told her plan, Peter Benari shook his head, and thought it would never do; but Tessa begged so hard, he consented at last that she should try it for one week, and sent her to bed the happiest little girl in New York.

Next morning the sun shone, but the cold wind blew, and the snow lay thick in the streets. As soon as her father was gone, Tessa flew about and put everything in nice order, telling the children she was going out for the day, and they were to mind Tommo's mother, who would see about the fire and the dinner; for the good woman loved Tessa, and entered into her little plans with all her heart. Nono and Giuseppe, or Sep, as they called him, wondered what she was going away for, and little Ranza cried at being left; but Tessa told them they would know all about it in a week, and have a fine time if they were good; so they kissed her all round and let her go.

Poor Tessa's heart beat fast as she trudged away with Tommo, who slung his harp over his shoulder, and gave her his hand. It was rather a dirty hand, but so kind that Tessa clung to it, and kept looking up at the friendly brown face for encouragement.

"We go first to the *café*, where many French and Italians eat the breakfast. They like my music, and often give me sips of hot coffee, which I like much. You too shall have the sips, and perhaps the pennies, for these people are greatly kind," said Tommo, leading her into a large smoky place where many people sat at little tables, eating and drinking. "See, now, have no fear; give them 'Bella Monica'; that is merry and will make the laugh," whispered Tommo, tuning his harp.

For a moment Tessa felt so frightened that she wanted to run away; but she remembered the empty stockings at home, and the fine plan, and she resolved *not* to give it up. One fat old Frenchman nodded to her, and it seemed to help her very much; for she began to sing before she thought, and that was the hardest part of it. Her voice trembled, and her cheeks grew redder and redder as she went on; but she kept her eyes fixed on her old shoes, and so got through without breaking down, which was very nice. The people laughed, for the song *was* merry; and the fat man smiled and nodded again. This gave her courage to try another, and she sung better and better each time; for Tommo played his best, and kept whispering to her, "Yes; we go well; this is fine. They will give the money and the blessed coffee."

So they did; for, when the little concert was over, several men put pennies in the cap Tessa offered, and the fat man took her on his knee, and ordered a mug of coffee, and some bread and butter for them both. This quite won her heart; and when they left the *café*, she kissed her hand to the old Frenchman, and said to her friend, "How kind they are! I like this very much; and now it is not hard."

But Tommo shook his curly head, and answered, soberly, "Yes, I took you there first, for they love music, and are of our country; but up among the great houses we shall not always do well. The people there are busy or hard or idle, and care nothing for harps and songs. Do not skip and laugh too soon; for the day is long, and we have but twelve pennies yet."

Tessa walked more quietly, and rubbed her cold hands, feeling that the world was a very big place, and wondering how the children got on at home without the little mother. Till noon they did not earn much, for every one seemed in a hurry, and the noise of many sleigh-bells drowned the music. Slowly they made their way up to the great squares where the big houses were, with fine ladies and pretty children at the windows. Here Tessa sung all her best songs, and Tommo played as fast as his fingers could fly; but it was too cold to have the windows open, so the pretty children could not listen long, and the ladies tossed out a little money, and soon went back to their own affairs.

All the afternoon the two friends wandered about, singing and playing, and gathering up their small harvest. At dusk they went home, Tessa so hoarse she could hardly speak, and so tired she fell asleep over her supper. But she had made half a dollar, for Tommo divided the money fairly, and she felt rich with her share. The other days were very much like this; sometimes they made more, sometimes less, but Tommo always "went halves"; and Tessa kept on, in spite of cold and weariness, for her plans grew as her earnings increased, and now she hoped to get useful things, instead of candy and toys alone.

On the day before Christmas, she made herself as tidy as she could, for she hoped to earn a good deal. She tied a bright scarlet handkerchief over the old hood, and the brilliant color set off her brown cheeks and bright eyes, as well as the pretty black braids of her hair. Tommo's mother lent her a pair of boots so big that they turned up at the toes, but there were no holes in them, and Tessa felt quite elegant in whole boots. Her hands were covered with chilblains, for she had no mittens; but she put them under her shawl, and scuffled merrily away in her big boots, feeling so glad that the week was over, and nearly three dollars safe in her pocket. How gay the streets were that day! how brisk every one was, and how bright the faces looked, as people trotted about with big baskets, holly-wreaths, and young evergreens going to blossom into splendid Christmas trees!

"If I could have a tree for the children, I'd never want anything again. But I can't; so I'll fill the socks all full, and be happy," said Tessa, as she looked wistfully into the gay stores, and saw the heavy baskets go by.

"Who knows what may happen if we do well?" returned Tommo, nodding wisely, for he had a plan as well as Tessa, and kept chuckling over it as he trudged through the mud. They did *not* do well somehow, for every one seemed so full of their own affairs they could not stop to listen, even to "Bella Monica," but bustled away to spend their money in turkeys, toys, and trees. In the afternoon it began to rain, and poor Tessa's heart to fail her; for the big boots tired her feet, the cold wind made her hands ache, and the rain spoilt the fine red handkerchief. Even Tommo looked sober, and didn't whistle as he walked, for he also was disappointed, and his plan looked rather doubtful, the pennies came in so slowly.

"We'll try one more street, and then go home, thou art so tired, little one. Come; let me wipe thy face, and give me thy hand here in my jacket pocket; there it will be as warm as any kitten"; and kind Tommo brushed away the drops which were not *all* rain from Tessa's cheeks, tucked the poor hand into his ragged pocket, and led her carefully along the slippery streets, for the boots nearly tripped her up.

## II.

At the first house, a cross old gentleman flapped his newspaper at them; at the second, a young gentleman and lady were so busy talking that they never turned their heads, and at the third, a servant came out and told them to go away, because some one was sick. At the fourth, some people let them sing all their songs and gave nothing. The next three houses were empty; and the last of all showed not a single face as they looked up anxiously. It was so cold, so dark and discouraging, that Tessa couldn't help one sob; and, as he glanced down at the little red nose and wet figure beside him, Tommo gave his harp an angry thump, and said something very fierce in Italian. They were just going to turn away; but they didn't, for that angry thump happened to be the best thing they could have done. All of a sudden a little head appeared at the window, as if the sound had brought it; then another and another, till there were five, of all heights and colors, and five eager faces peeped out, smiling and nodding to the two below.

"Sing, Tessa; sing! Quick! quick!" cried Tommo, twanging away with all his might, and showing his white teeth, as he smiled back at the little gentle-folk.

Bless us! How Tessa did tune up at that! She chirped away like a real bird, forgetting all about the tears on her cheeks, the ache in her hands, and the heaviness at her heart. The children laughed, and clapped their hands, and cried "More! more! Sing another, little girl! Please do!" And away they went again, piping and playing, till Tessa's breath was gone, and Tommo's stout fingers tingled well.

"Mamma says, come to the door; it's too muddy to throw the money into the street!" cried out a kindly child's voice as Tessa held up the old cap, with beseeching eyes.

Up the wide stone steps went the street musicians, and the whole flock came running down to give a handful of silver, and ask all sorts of questions. Tessa felt so grateful that, without waiting for Tommo, she sang her sweetest little song all alone. It was about a lost lamb, and her heart was in the song; therefore she sang it well, so well that a pretty young lady came down to listen, and stood watching the bright-eyed girl, who looked about her as she sang, evidently enjoying the light and warmth of the fine hall, and the sight of the lovely children with their gay dresses, shining hair, and dainty little shoes.

"You have a charming voice, child. Who taught you to sing?" asked the young lady kindly.

"My mother. She is dead now; but I do not forget," answered Tessa, in her pretty broken English.

"I wish she could sing at our tree, since Bella is ill," cried one of the children peeping through the banisters.

"She is not fair enough for the angel, and too large to go up in the tree. But she sings sweetly, and looks as if she would like to see a tree," said the young lady.

"Oh, so much!" exclaimed Tessa; adding eagerly, "my sister Ranza is small and pretty as a baby-angel. She could sit up in the fine tree, and I could sing for her from under the table."

"Sit down and warm yourself, and tell me about Ranza," said the kind elder sister, who liked the confiding little girl, in spite of her shabby clothes.

So Tessa sat down and dried the big boots over the furnace, and told her story, while Tommo stood modestly in the background, and the children listened with faces full of interest.

"O Rose! let us see the little girl; and if she will do, let us have her, and Tessa can learn our song, and it will be splendid!" cried the biggest boy, who sat astride of a chair, and stared at the harp with round eyes.

"I'll ask mamma," said Rose; and away she went into the dining-room close by. As the door opened, Tessa saw what looked to her like a fairy feast—all silver mugs and flowery plates and oranges and nuts and rosy wine in tall glass pitchers, and smoking dishes that smelt so deliciously she could not restrain a little sniff of satisfaction.

"Are you hungry?" asked the boy in a grand tone.

"Yes, sir," meekly answered Tessa.

"I say, mamma; she wants something to eat. Can I give her an orange?" called the boy, prancing away into the splendid room, quite like a fairy prince, Tessa thought.

A plump motherly lady came out and looked at Tessa, asked a few questions, and then told her to come to-morrow with Ranza, and they would see what could be done. Tessa clapped her hands for joy—she didn't mind the chilblains now—and Tommo played a lively march, he was so pleased.

"Will you come, too, and bring your harp? You shall be paid, and shall have something from the tree, likewise," said the motherly lady, who liked what Tessa gratefully told about his kindness to her.

"Ah, yes; I shall come with much gladness, and play as never in my life before," cried Tommo, with a flourish of the old cap that made the children laugh.

"Give these to your brothers," said the fairy prince, stuffing nuts and oranges into Tessa's hands.

"And these to the little girl," added one of the young princesses, flying out of the dining-room with cakes and rosy apples for Ranza.

Tessa didn't know what to say; but her eyes were full, and she just took the mother's white hand in both her little grimy ones, and kissed it many times in her pretty Italian fashion. The lady understood her, and stroked her cheek softly, saying to her elder daughter, "We must take care of this good little creature. Freddy, bring me your mittens; these poor hands must be covered. Alice, get your play-hood; this handkerchief is all wet; and, Maud, bring the old chinchilla tippet."

The children ran, and in a minute there were lovely blue mittens on the red hands, a warm hood over the black braids, and a soft "pussy" round the sore throat.

"Ah! so kind, so very kind! I have no way to say 'thank you'; but Ranza shall be for you a heavenly angel, and I will sing my heart out for your tree!" cried Tessa, folding the mittens as if she would say a prayer of thankfulness if she knew how.

Then they went away, and the pretty children called after them, "Come again, Tessa! come again, Tommo!" Now the rain didn't seem dismal, the wind cold, nor the way long, as they bought their gifts and hurried home, for kind words and the sweet magic of charity had changed all the world to them.

I think the good spirits who fly about on Christmas Eve, to help the loving fillers of little stockings, smiled very kindly on Tessa as she brooded joyfully over the small store of presents that seemed so magnificent to her. All the goodies were divided evenly into three parts and stowed away in father's three big socks, which hung against the curtain. With her three dollars, she had got a pair of shoes for Nono, a knit cap for Sep, and a pair of white stockings for Ranza; to her she also gave the new hood; to Nono the mittens; and to Sep the tippet.

"Now the dear boys can go out, and my Ranza will be ready for the lady to see, in her nice new things," said Tessa, quite sighing with pleasure to see how well the gifts looked pinned up beside the bulging socks, which wouldn't hold them all. The little mother kept nothing for herself but the pleasure of giving everything away; yet, I think, she was both richer and happier than if she had kept them all. Her father laughed as he had not done since the mother died, when he saw how comically the old curtain had broken out into boots and hoods, stockings and tippets.

"I wish I had a gold gown and a silver hat for thee, my Tessa, thou art so good. May the saints bless and keep thee always!" said Peter Benari tenderly, as he held his little daughter close and gave her the good-night kiss.

Tessa felt very rich as she crept under the faded counterpane, feeling as if she had received a lovely gift, and fell happily asleep with chubby Ranza in her arms, and the two rough black heads peeping out at the foot of the bed. She dreamed wonderful dreams that night, and woke in the morning to find real wonders before her eyes. She got up early to see if the socks were all right, and there she found the most astonishing sight. Four socks, instead of three; and by the fourth, pinned out quite elegantly, was a little dress, evidently meant for her—a warm, woollen dress, all made, and actually with bright buttons on it. It nearly took her breath away; so did the new boots on the floor, and the funny long stocking like a grey sausage, with a wooden doll staring out at the top, as if she said, politely, "A Merry Christmas, ma'am!" Tessa screamed and danced in her delight, and up tumbled all the children to scream and dance with her, making a regular carnival on a small scale. Everybody hugged and kissed everybody else, offered sucks of orange, bites of cake, and exchanges of candy; every one tried on the new things and pranced about in them like a flock of peacocks. Ranza skipped to and fro airily, dressed in her white socks and the red hood; the boys promenaded in their little shirts, one with his creaking new shoes and mittens, the other in his gay cap and fine tippet; and Tessa put her dress straight on, feeling that her father's "gold gown" was not all a joke. In her long stocking she found all sorts of treasures; for Tommo had stuffed it full of queer things, and his mother had made gingerbread into every imaginable shape, from fat pigs to full omnibuses.

Dear me! What happy little souls they were that morning; and when they were quiet again, how like a fairy tale did Tessa's story sound to them. Ranza was quite ready to be an angel; and the boys promised to be marvellously good, if they were only allowed to see the tree at the "palace," as they called the great house.

Little Ranza was accepted with delight by the kind lady and her children, and Tessa learned the song quite easily. The boys *were* asked; and, after a happy day, the young Italians all returned, to play their parts at the fine Christmas party. Mamma and Miss Rose drilled them all; and when the folding-doors flew open, one rapturous "Oh!" arose from the crowd of children gathered to the festival. I assure you, it was splendid; the great tree glittering with lights and gifts; and, on her invisible perch, up among the green boughs, sat the little golden-haired angel, all in white, with downy wings, a shining crown on her head, and the most serene satisfaction in her blue eyes, as she stretched her chubby arms to those below, and smiled her baby smile at them. Before any one could speak, a voice, as fresh and sweet as a lark's, sang the Christmas Carol so blithely that every one stood still to hear, and then clapped till the little angel shook on her perch, and cried out, "Be 'till, or me'll fall!" How they laughed at that; and what fun they had talking to Ranza, while Miss Rose stripped the tree, for the angel could not resist temptation, and amused herself by eating all the bonbons she could reach, till she was taken down, to dance about like a fairy in a white frock and red shoes. Tessa and her friends had many presents; the boys were perfect lambs, Tommo played for the little folks to dance, and every one said something friendly to the strangers, so that they did not feel shy, in spite of shabby clothes. It was a happy night: and all their lives they remembered it as something too beautiful and bright to be quite true. Before they went home, the kind mamma told Tessa she should be her friend, and gave her a motherly kiss, which warmed the child's heart and seemed to set a seal upon that promise. It was faithfully kept, for the rich lady had been touched by Tessa's patient struggles and sacrifices; and for many years, thanks to her benevolence, there was no end to Tessa's Surprises.

L. M. MONTGOMERY

1874-1942

# THE CHRISTMAS SURPRISE
# AT ENDERLY ROAD

"Phil, I'm getting fearfully hungry. When are we going to strike civilization?"

The speaker was my chum, Frank Ward. We were home from our academy for the Christmas holidays and had been amusing ourselves on this sunshiny December afternoon by a tramp through the "back lands," as the barrens that swept away south behind the village were called. They were grown over with scrub maple and spruce, and were quite pathless save for meandering sheep tracks that crossed and re-crossed, but led apparently nowhere.

Frank and I did not know exactly where we were,

but the back lands were not so extensive but that we would come out somewhere if we kept on. It was getting late and we wished to go home.

"I have an idea that we ought to strike civilization somewhere up the Enderly Road pretty soon," I answered.

"Do you call *that* civilization?" said Frank, with a laugh.

No Blackburn Hill boy was ever known to miss an opportunity of flinging a slur at Enderly Road, even if no Enderly Roader were by to feel the sting.

Enderly Road was a miserable little settlement straggling back from Blackburn Hill. It was a forsaken looking place, and the people, as a rule, were poor and shiftless. Between Blackburn Hill and Enderly Road very little social intercourse existed and, as the Road people resented what they called the pride of Blackburn Hill, there was a good deal of bad feeling between the two districts.

Presently Frank and I came out on the Enderly Road. We sat on the fence a few minutes to rest and discuss our route home. "If we go by the road it's three miles," said Frank. "Isn't there a short cut?"

"There ought to be one by the wood-lane that comes out by Jacob Hart's," I answered, "but I don't know where to strike it."

"Here is someone coming now; we'll inquire," said Frank, looking up the curve of the hard-frozen road. The "someone" was a little girl of about ten years old, who was trotting along with a basketful of school books on her arm. She was a pale, pinched little thing, and her jacket and red hood seemed very old and thin.

"Hello, missy," I said, as she came up, and then I stopped, for I saw she had been crying.

"What is the matter?" asked Frank, who was much more at ease with children than I was, and had always a warm spot in his heart for their small troubles. "Has your teacher kept you in for being naughty?"

The mite dashed her little red knuckles across her eyes and answered indignantly, "No, indeed. I stayed after school with Minnie Lawler to sweep the floor."

"And did you and Minnie quarrel, and is that why you are crying?" asked Frank solemnly.

"Minnie and I *never* quarrel. I am crying because

we can't have the school decorated on Monday for the examination, after all. The Dickeys have gone back on us . . . after promising, too," and the tears began to swell up in the blue eyes again.

"Very bad behaviour on the part of the Dickeys," commented Frank. "But can't you decorate the school without them?"

"Why, of course not. They are the only big boys in the school. They said they would cut the boughs, and bring a ladder tomorrow and help us nail the wreaths up, and now they won't . . . and everything is spoiled . . . and Miss Davis will be so disappointed."

By dint of questioning Frank soon found out the whole story. The semi-annual public examination was to be held on Monday afternoon, the day before Christmas. Miss Davis had been drilling her little flock for the occasion; and a program of recitations, speeches, and dialogues had been prepared. Our small informant, whose name was Maggie Bates, together with Minnie Lawler and several other little girls, had conceived the idea that it would be a fine thing to decorate the schoolroom with greens. For this it was necessary to ask the help of the boys.

Boys were scarce at Enderly school, but the Dickeys, three in number, had promised to see that the thing was done.

"And now they won't," sobbed Maggie. "Matt Dickey is mad at Miss Davis 'cause she stood him on the floor today for not learning his lesson, and he says he won't do a thing nor let any of the other boys help us. Matt just makes all the boys do as he says. I feel dreadful bad, and so does Minnie."

"Well, I wouldn't cry any more about it," said Frank consolingly. "Crying won't do any good, you know. Can you tell us where to find the wood-lane that cuts across to Blackburn Hill?" Maggie could, and gave us minute directions. So, having thanked her, we left her to pursue her disconsolate way and betook ourselves homeward.

"I would like to spoil Matt Dickey's little game," said Frank. "He is evidently trying to run things at Enderly Road school and revenge himself on the teacher. Let us put a spoke in his wheel and do Maggie a good turn as well."

".Agreed. But how?"

Frank had a plan ready to hand and, when we

reached home, we took his sisters, Carrie and Mabel, into our confidence; and the four of us worked to such good purpose all the next day, which was Saturday, that by night everything was in readiness.

At dusk Frank and I set out for the Enderly Road, carrying a basket, a small step-ladder, an unlit lantern, a hammer, and a box of tacks. It was dark when we reached the Enderly Road schoolhouse. Fortunately, it was quite out of sight of any inhabited spot, being surrounded by woods. Hence, mysterious lights in it at strange hours would not be likely to attract attention.

The door was locked, but we easily got in by a window, lighted our lantern, and went to work. The schoolroom was small, and the old-fashioned furniture bore marks of hard usage; but everything was very snug, and the carefully swept floor and dusted desks bore testimony to the neatness of our small friend Maggie and her chum Minnie.

Our basket was full of mottoes made from letters cut out of cardboard and covered with lissome sprays of fir. They were, moreover, adorned with gorgeous pink and red tissue roses, which Carrie and

Mabel had contributed. We had considerable trouble in getting them tacked up properly, but when we had succeeded, and had furthermore surmounted doors, windows, and blackboard with wreaths of green, the little Enderly Road schoolroom was quite transformed.

"It looks nice," said Frank in a tone of satisfaction. "Hope Maggie will like it."

We swept up the litter we had made, and then scrambled out of the window.

"I'd like to see Matt Dickey's face when he comes Monday morning," I laughed, as we struck into the back lands.

"I'd like to see that midget of a Maggie's," said Frank. "See here, Phil, let's attend the examination Monday afternoon. I'd like to see our decorations in daylight."

We decided to do so, and also thought of something else. Snow fell all day Sunday, so that, on Monday morning, sleighs had to be brought out. Frank and I drove down to the store and invested a considerable share of our spare cash in a varied assortment of knick-knacks. After dinner we drove through to the Enderly Road schoolhouse, tied our horse in a quiet spot, and went in. Our arrival created quite a sensation for, as a rule, Blackburn Hillites did not patronize Enderly Road functions. Miss Davis, the pale, tired-looking little teacher, was evidently pleased, and we were given seats of honour next to the minister on the platform.

Our decorations really looked very well, and were further enhanced by two large red geraniums in full bloom which, it appeared, Maggie had brought from home to adorn the teacher's desk. The side benches were lined with Enderly Road parents, and all the pupils were in their best attire. Our friend Maggie was there, of course, and she smiled and nodded towards the wreaths when she caught our eyes.

The examination was a decided success, and the program which followed was very creditable indeed. Maggie and Minnie, in particular, covered themselves with glory, both in class and on the platform. At its close, while the minister was making his speech, Frank slipped out; when the minister sat down, the door opened and Santa Claus himself, with big fur coat, ruddy mask, and long white beard, strode into the room with a huge basket on his arm, amid a chorus of surprised "Ohs" from old and young.

Wonderful things came out of that basket. There was some little present for every child there—tops, knives, and whistles for the boys, dolls and ribbons for the girls, and a "prize" box of candy for everybody, all of which Santa Claus presented with appropriate remarks. It was an exciting time, and it would have been hard to decide which were the most pleased, parents, pupils, or teacher.

In the confusion Santa Claus discreetly disappeared, and school was dismissed. Frank, having tucked his toggery away in the sleigh, was waiting for us outside, and we were promptly pounced upon by Maggie and Minnie, whose long braids were already adorned with the pink silk ribbons which had been their gifts.

"*You* decorated the school," cried Maggie excitedly. "I know you did. I told Minnie it was you the minute I saw it."

"You're dreaming, child," said Frank.

"Oh, no, I'm not," retorted Maggie shrewdly, "and wasn't Matt Dickey mad this morning! Oh, it was such fun. I think you are two real nice boys and so does Minnie—don't you, Minnie?"

Minnie nodded gravely. Evidently Maggie did the talking in their partnership.

"This has been a splendid examination," said Maggie, drawing a long breath. "Real Christmassy, you know. We never had such a good time before."

"Well, it has paid, don't you think?" asked Frank, as we drove home.

"Rather," I answered.

It did "pay" in other ways than the mere pleasure of it. There was always a better feeling between the Roaders and the Hillites thereafter. The big brothers of the little girls, to whom our Christmas surprise had been such a treat, thought it worthwhile to bury the hatchet, and quarrels between the two villages became things of the past.

# CLORINDA'S GIFTS

"It is a dreadful thing to be poor a fortnight before Christmas," said Clorinda, with the mournful sigh of seventeen years.

Aunt Emmy smiled. Aunt Emmy was sixty, and spent the hours she didn't spend in a bed, on a sofa or in a wheel chair; but Aunt Emmy was never heard to sigh.

"I suppose it is worse then than at any other time," she admitted.

That was one of the nice things about Aunt Emmy. She always sympathized and understood.

"I'm worse than poor this Christmas . . . I'm stony broke," said Clorinda dolefully. "My spell of fever in the summer and the consequent doctor's bills have cleaned out my coffers completely. Not a single Christmas present can I give. And I did so want to give some little thing to each of my dearest people. But I simply can't afford it . . . that's the hateful, ugly truth."

Clorinda sighed again.

"The gifts which money can purchase are not the only ones we can give," said Aunt Emmy gently, "nor the best, either."

"Oh, I know it's nicer to give something of your own work," agreed Clorinda, "but materials for fancy work cost too. That kind of gift is just as much out of the question for me as any other."

"That was not what I meant," said Aunt Emmy.

"What did you mean, then?" asked Clorinda, looking puzzled.

Aunt Emmy smiled.

"Suppose you think out my meaning for yourself," she said. "That would be better than if I explained it. Besides, I don't think I *could* explain it. Take the beautiful line of a beautiful poem to help you in your thinking out: 'The gift without the giver is bare.'"

"I'd put it the other way and say, 'The giver without the gift is bare,'" said Clorinda, with a grimace. "That is my predicament exactly. Well, I hope by next Christmas I'll not be quite bankrupt. I'm going into Mr. Callender's store down at Murraybridge in February. He has offered me the place, you know."

"Won't your aunt miss you terribly?" said Aunt Emmy gravely.

Clorinda flushed. There was a note in Aunt Emmy's voice that disturbed her.

"Oh, yes, I suppose she will," she answered hurriedly. "But she'll get used to it very soon. And I will be home every Saturday night, you know. I'm dreadfully tired of being poor, Aunt Emmy, and now that I have a chance to earn something for myself I mean to take it. I can help Aunt Mary, too. I'm to get four dollars a week."

"I think she would rather have your companionship than a part of your salary, Clorinda," said Aunt Emmy. "But of course you must decide for yourself, dear. It is hard to be poor. I know it. I am poor."

"You poor!" said Clorinda, kissing her. "Why, you are the richest woman I know, Aunt Emmy—rich in love and goodness and contentment."

"And so are you, dearie . . . rich in youth and health and happiness and ambition. Aren't they all worth while?"

"Of course they are," laughed Clorinda. "Only, unfortunately, Christmas gifts can't be coined out of them."

"Did you ever try?" asked Aunt Emmy. "Think out that question, too, in your thinking out, Clorinda."

"Well, I must say bye-bye and run home. I feel cheered up—you always cheer people up, Aunt Emmy. How grey it is outdoors. I do hope we'll have snow soon. Wouldn't it be jolly to have a white Christmas? We always have such faded brown Decembers."

Clorinda lived just across the road from Aunt Emmy in a tiny white house behind some huge willows. But Aunt Mary lived there too—the only relative Clorinda had, for Aunt Emmy wasn't really her aunt at all. Clorinda had always lived with Aunt Mary ever since she could remember.

Clorinda went home and upstairs to her little room under the eaves, where the great bare willow boughs were branching athwart her windows. She was thinking over what Aunt Emmy had said about Christmas gifts and giving.

"I'm sure I don't know what she could have meant," pondered Clorinda. "I do wish I could find out if it would help me any. I'd love to remember a few of my friends at least. There's Miss Mitchell . . . she's been so good to me all this year and helped me so much with my studies. And there's Mrs. Martin out in Manitoba. If I could only send her something! She must be so lonely out there. And Aunt Emmy herself, of course; and poor old Aunt Kitty down the lane; and Aunt Mary and, yes—Florence too, although she did treat me so meanly. I shall never feel the same to her again. But she gave me a present last Christmas, and so out of mere politeness I ought to give her something."

Clorinda stopped short suddenly. She had just remembered that she would not have liked to say that last sentence to Aunt Emmy. Therefore, there was something wrong about it. Clorinda had long ago learned that there was sure to be something wrong in anything that could not be said to Aunt Emmy. So she stopped to think it over.

Clorinda puzzled over Aunt Emmy's meaning for four days and part of three nights. Then all at once it came to her. Or if it wasn't Aunt Emmy's meaning it was a very good meaning in itself, and it grew clearer and expanded in meaning during the days that followed, although at first Clorinda shrank a little from some of the conclusions to which it led her.

"I've solved the problem of my Christmas giving for this year," she told Aunt Emmy. "I have some things to give after all. Some of them quite costly, too; that is, they will cost me something, but I know I'll be better off and richer after I've paid the price. That is what Mr. Grierson would call a paradox, isn't it? I'll explain all about it to you on Christmas Day."

On Christmas Day, Clorinda went over to Aunt Emmy's. It was a faded brown Christmas after all, for the snow had not come. But Clorinda did not mind; there was such joy in her heart that she thought it the most delightful Christmas Day that ever dawned.

She put the queer cornery armful she carried down on the kitchen floor before she went into the sitting room. Aunt Emmy was lying on the sofa before the fire, and Clorinda sat down beside her.

"I've come to tell you all about it," she said.

Aunt Emmy patted the hand that was in her own.

"From your face, dear girl, it will be pleasant hearing and telling," she said.

Clorinda nodded.

"Aunt Emmy, I thought for days over your meaning . . . thought until I was dizzy. And then one evening it just came to me, without any thinking at all, and I knew that I could give some gifts after all. I thought of something new every day for a week. At first I didn't think I *could* give some of them, and then I thought how selfish I was. I would have been willing to pay any amount of money for gifts if I had had it, but I wasn't willing to pay what I had. I got over that, though, Aunt Emmy. Now I'm going to tell you what I did give.

"First, there was my teacher, Miss Mitchell. I gave her one of father's books. I have so many of his, you know, so that I wouldn't miss one; but still it was one I loved very much, and so I felt that that love made it worth while. That is, I felt that on second thought. At first, Aunt Emmy, I thought I would be ashamed to offer Miss Mitchell a shabby old book, worn with much reading and all marked over with father's notes and pencillings. I was afraid she would think it queer of me to give her such a present. And yet somehow it seemed to me that it was better than something brand new and unmellowed—that old book which father had loved and which I loved. So I gave it to her, and she understood. I think it pleased her so much, the real meaning in it. She said it was like being given something out of another's heart and life.

"Then you know Mrs. Martin . . . last year she was Miss Hope, my dear Sunday School teacher. She married a home missionary, and they are in a lonely part of the west. Well, I wrote her a letter. Not just an ordinary letter; dear me, no. I took a whole day to write it, and you should have seen the postmistress's eyes stick out when I mailed it. I just told her everything that had happened in Greenvale since she went away. I made it as newsy and cheerful and loving as I possibly could. Everything bright and funny I could think of went into it.

"The next was old Aunt Kitty. You know she was my nurse when I was a baby, and she's very fond of me. But, well, you know, Aunt Emmy, I'm ashamed to confess it, but really I've never found Aunt Kitty very entertaining, to put it mildly. She is always glad when I go to see her, but I've never gone except when I couldn't help it. She is very deaf, and rather dull and stupid, you know. Well, I gave her a whole day. I took my knitting yesterday, and sat with her the whole time and just talked and talked. I told her all the Greenvale news and gossip and everything else I thought she'd like to hear. She was so pleased and proud; she told me when I came away that she hadn't had such a nice time for years.

"Then there was . . . Florence. You know, Aunt Emmy, we were always intimate friends until last year. Then Florence once told Rose Watson something I had told her in confidence. I found it out and I was so hurt. I couldn't forgive Florence, and I told her plainly I could never be a real friend to her again. Florence felt badly, because she really did love me, and she asked me to forgive her, but it seemed as if I couldn't. Well, Aunt Emmy, that was my Christmas gift to her . . . my forgiveness. I went down last night and just put my arms around her and told her that I loved her as much as ever and wanted to be real close friends again.

"I gave Aunt Mary her gift this morning. I told her I wasn't going to Murraybridge, that I just meant to stay home with her. She was so glad—and I'm glad, too, now that I've decided so."

"Your gifts have been real gifts, Clorinda," said Aunt Emmy. "Something of you—the best of you—went into each of them."

Clorinda went out and brought her cornery armful in.

"I didn't forget you, Aunt Emmy," she said, as she unpinned the paper.

There was a rosebush—Clorinda's own pet rosebush—all snowed over with fragrant blossoms.

Aunt Emmy loved flowers. She put her finger under one of the roses and kissed it.

"It's as sweet as yourself, dear child," she said tenderly. "And it will be a joy to me all through the lonely winter days. You've found out the best meaning of Christmas giving, haven't you, dear?"

"Yes, thanks to you, Aunt Emmy," said Clorinda softly.

# HANS CHRISTIAN ANDERSEN

1805-1875

# THE FIR TREE

Far away in the forest, where the warm sun and the fresh air made a sweet resting place, grew a pretty little fir tree. The situation was all that could be desired; and yet the tree was not happy, it wished so much to be like its tall companions, the pines and firs which grew around it.

The sun shone, and the soft air fluttered its leaves, and the little peasant children passed by, prattling merrily; but the fir tree did not heed them.

Sometimes the children would bring a large basket of raspberries or strawberries, wreathed on straws, and seat themselves near the fir tree, and say, "Is it not a pretty little tree?" which made it feel even more unhappy than before.

And yet all this while the tree grew a notch or joint taller every year, for by the number of joints in the stem of a fir tree we can discover its age.

Still, as it grew, it complained: "Oh! how I wish I were as tall as the other trees; then I would spread out my branches on every side, and my crown would overlook the wide world around. I should have the birds building their nests on my boughs, and when the wind blew, I should bow with stately dignity, like my tall companions."

So discontented was the tree, that it took no pleasure in the warm sunshine, the birds, or the rosy clouds that floated over it morning and evening.

Sometimes in winter, when the snow lay white and glittering on the ground, there was a little hare that would come springing along, and jump right over the little tree's head; then how mortified it would feel.

Two winters passed; and when the third arrived, the tree had grown so tall that the hare was obliged to run round it. Yet it remained unsatisfied and would exclaim: "Oh! to grow, to grow; if I could but keep on growing tall and old! There is nothing else worth caring for in the world."

In the autumn the woodcutters came, as usual, and cut down several of the tallest trees; and the young fir, which was now grown to a good, full height, shuddered as the noble trees fell to the earth with a crash.

After the branches were lopped off, the trunks looked so slender and bare that they could scarcely be recognized. Then they were placed, one upon another, upon wagons and drawn by horses out of the forest. Where could they be going? What would become of them? The young fir tree wished very much to know.

So in the spring, when the swallows and the storks came, it asked: "Do you know where those trees were taken? Did you meet them?"

The swallows knew nothing; but the stork, after a little reflection, nodded his head and said: "Yes, I think I do. As I flew from Egypt, I met several new ships, and they had fine masts that smelt like fir. These must have been the trees; and I assure you they were stately; they sailed right gloriously!"

"Oh, how I wish I were tall enough to go on the sea," said the fir tree. "Tell me what is this sea, and what does it look like?"

"It would take too much time to explain—a great deal too much," said the stork, flying quickly away.

"Rejoice in thy youth," said the sunbeam; "rejoice in thy fresh growth and in the young life that is in thee."

And the wind kissed the tree, and the dew watered it with tears, but the fir tree regarded them not.

Christmas time drew near, and many young trees were cut down, some that were even smaller and younger than the fir tree, who enjoyed neither rest nor peace for longing to leave its forest home. These young trees, which were chosen for their beauty, kept their branches, and they, also, were laid on wagons and drawn by horses far away out of the forest.

"Where are they going?" asked the fir tree. "They are not taller than I am; indeed, one is not so tall. And why do they keep all their branches? Where are they going?"

"We know, we know," sang the sparrows; "we

have looked in at the windows of the houses in the town, and we know what is done with them. Oh! you cannot think what honor and glory they receive. They are dressed up in the most splendid manner. We have seen them standing in the middle of a warm room, and adorned with all sorts of beautiful things—honey cakes, gilded apples, playthings, and many hundreds of wax tapers."

"And then," asked the fir tree, trembling in all its branches, "and then what happens?"

"We did not see any more," said the sparrows; "but this was enough for us."

"I wonder whether anything so brilliant will ever happen to me," thought the fir tree. "It would be better even than crossing the sea. I long for it almost with pain. Oh, when will Christmas be here? I am now as tall and well grown as those which were taken away last year. O that I were now laid on the wagon, or standing in the warm room with all that brightness and splendor around me! Something better and more beautiful is to come after, or the trees would not be so decked out. Yes, what follows will be grander and more splendid. What can it be? I am weary with longing. I scarcely know what it is that I feel."

"Rejoice in our love," said the air and the sunlight. "Enjoy thine own bright life in the fresh air."

But the tree would not rejoice, though it grew taller every day, and winter and summer its dark-green foliage might be seen in the forest, while passers-by would say, "What a beautiful tree!"

A short time before the next Christmas the discontented fir tree was the first to fall. As the ax cut sharply through the stem and divided the pith, the tree fell with a groan to the earth, conscious of pain and faintness and forgetting all its dreams of happiness in sorrow at leaving its home in the forest. It knew that it should never again see its dear old companions the trees, nor the little bushes and many-colored flowers that had grown by its side; perhaps not even the birds. Nor was the journey at all pleasant.

The tree first recovered itself while being unpacked in the courtyard of a house, with several other trees; and it heard a man say: "We only want one, and this is the prettiest. This is beautiful!"

Then came two servants in grand livery and carried the fir tree into a large and beautiful apartment. Pictures hung on the walls, and near the tall tile stove stood great china vases with lions on the lids. There were rocking-chairs, silken sofas, and large tables covered with pictures; and there were books, and playthings that had cost a hundred times a hundred dollars—at least so said the children.

Then the fir tree was placed in a large tub full of sand—but green baize hung all round it so that no one could know it was a tub—and it stood on a very handsome carpet. Oh, how the fir tree trembled! What was going to happen to him now? Some young ladies came, and the servants helped them to adorn the tree.

On one branch they hung little bags cut out of colored paper, and each bag was filled with sweetmeats. From other branches hung gilded apples and walnuts, as if they had grown there; and above and all around were hundreds of red, blue, and white tapers, which were fastened upon the branches. Dolls, exactly like real men and women, were placed under the green leaves—the tree had never seen such things before—and at the very top was fastened a glittering star made of gold tinsel. Oh, it was very beautiful. "This evening," they all exclaimed, "how bright it will be!"

"O that the evening were come," thought the tree, "and the tapers lighted! Then I shall know what else is going to happen. Will the trees of the forest come to see me? Will the sparrows peep in at the windows, I wonder, as they fly? Shall I grow faster here than in the forest, and shall I keep on all these ornaments during summer and winter?" But guessing was of very little use. His back ached with trying, and this pain is as bad for a slender fir tree as headache is for us.

At last the tapers were lighted, and then what a glistening blaze of splendor the tree presented! It trembled so with joy in all its branches that one of the candles fell among the green leaves and burned some of them. "Help! help!" exclaimed the young ladies; but no harm was done, for they quickly extinguished the fire.

After this the tree tried not to tremble at all, though the fire frightened him, he was so anxious not to hurt any of the beautiful ornaments, even while their brilliancy dazzled him.

And now the folding doors were thrown open, and a troop of children rushed in as if they intended to upset the tree, and were followed more slowly by their elders. For a moment the little ones stood silent with astonishment, and then they shouted for joy till the room rang; and they danced merrily round the tree while one present after another was taken from it.

"What are they doing? What will happen next?" thought the tree. At last the candles burned down to the branches and were put out. Then the children received permission to plunder the tree.

Oh, how they rushed upon it! There was such a riot that the branches cracked, and had it not been fastened with the glistening star to the ceiling, it must have been thrown down.

Then the children danced about with their pretty toys, and no one noticed the tree except the children's maid, who came and peeped among the branches to see if an apple or a fig had been forgotten.

"A story, a story," cried the children, pulling a little fat man towards the tree.

"Now we shall be in the green shade," said the man as he seated himself under it, "and the tree will have the pleasure of hearing, also; but I shall only relate one story. What shall it be? Ivede-Avede or Humpty Dumpty, who fell downstairs, but soon got up again, and at last married a princess?"

"Ivede-Avede," cried some; "Humpty Dumpty," cried others; and there was a famous uproar. But the fir tree remained quite still and thought to himself: "Shall I have anything to do with all this? Ought I to make a noise, too?" but he had already amused them as much as they wished and they paid no attention to him.

Then the old man told them the story of Humpty Dumpty—how he fell downstairs, and was raised up again, and married a princess. And the children clapped their hands and cried, "Tell another, tell another," for they wanted to hear the story of Ivede-Avede; but this time they had only "Humpty Dumpty." After this the fir tree became quite silent and thoughtful. Never had the birds in the forest told such tales as that of Humpty Dumpty, who fell downstairs, and yet married a princess.

"Ah, yes! so it happens in the world," thought the fir tree. He believed it all, because it was related by such a pleasant man.

"Ah, well!" he thought, "who knows? Perhaps I may fall down, too, and marry a princess"; and he looked forward joyfully to the next evening, expecting to be again decked out with lights and playthings, gold and fruit. "To-morrow I will not tremble," thought he; "I will enjoy all my splendor, and I shall hear the story of Humpty Dumpty again, and perhaps of Ivede-Avede." And the tree remained quiet and thoughtful all night.

In the morning the servants and the housemaid came in. "Now," thought the fir tree, "all my splendor is going to begin again." But they dragged him out of the room and upstairs to the garret and threw him on the floor in a dark corner where no daylight shone, and there they left him. "What does this mean?" thought the tree. "What am I to do here? I can hear nothing in a place like this"; and he leaned against the wall and thought and thought.

And he had time enough to think, for days and nights passed and no one came near him; and when at last somebody did come, it was only to push away some large boxes in a corner. So the tree was completely hidden from sight, as if it had never existed.

"It is winter now," thought the tree; "the ground is hard and covered with snow, so that people cannot plant me. I shall be sheltered here, I dare say, until spring comes. How thoughtful and kind everybody is to me! Still, I wish this place were not so dark and so dreadfully lonely, with not even a little hare to look at. How pleasant it was out in the forest while the snow lay on the ground, when the hare would run by, yes, and jump over me, too, although I did not like it then. Oh! it is terribly lonely here."

"Squeak, squeak," said a little mouse, creeping cautiously towards the tree; then came another, and they both sniffed at the fir tree and crept in and out between the branches.

"Oh, it is very cold," said the little mouse. "If it were not we should be very comfortable here, shouldn't we, old fir tree?"

"I am not old," said the fir tree. "There are many who are older than I am."

"Where do you come from?" asked the mice, who were full of curiosity; "and what do you know? Have you seen the most beautiful places in the world, and can you tell us all about them? And have you been in the storeroom, where cheeses lie on the shelf and hams hang from the ceiling? One can run about on tallow candles there; one can go in thin and come out fat."

"I know nothing of that," said the fir tree, "but I know the wood, where the sun shines and the birds sing." And then the tree told the little mice all about its youth. They had never heard such an account in their lives; and after they had listened to it attentively, they said: "What a number of things you have seen! You must have been very happy."

"Happy!" exclaimed the fir tree; and then, as he reflected on what he had been telling them, he said, "Ah, yes! after all, those were happy days." But when he went on and related all about Christmas Eve, and how he had been dressed up with cakes and lights, the mice said, "How happy you must have been, you old fir tree."

"I am not old at all," replied the tree; "I only came from the forest this winter. I am now checked in my growth."

"What splendid stories you can tell," said the little mice. And the next night four other mice came with them to hear what the tree had to tell. The more he talked the more he remembered, and then he thought to himself: "Yes, those were happy days; but they may come again. Humpty Dumpty fell downstairs, and yet he married the princess. Perhaps I may marry a princess, too." And the fir tree thought of the pretty little birch tree that grew in the forest; a real princess, a beautiful princess, she was to him.

"Who is Humpty Dumpty?" asked the little mice. And then the tree related the whole story; he could remember every single word. And the little mice were so delighted with it that they were ready to jump to the top of the tree. The next night a great many more mice made their appearance, and on Sunday two rats came with them; but the rats said it was not a pretty story at all, and the little mice were very sorry, for it made them also think less of it.

"Do you know only that one story?" asked the rats.

"Only that one," replied the fir tree. "I heard it on the happiest evening in my life; but I did not know I was so happy at the time."

"We think it is a very miserable story," said the rats. "Don't you know any story about bacon or tallow in the storeroom?"

"No," replied the tree.

"Many thanks to you, then," replied the rats, and they went their ways.

The little mice also kept away after this, and the tree sighed and said: "It was very pleasant when the merry little mice sat round me and listened while I talked. Now that is all past, too. However, I shall consider myself happy when some one comes to take me out of this place."

But would this ever happen? Yes; one morning people came to clear up the garret; the boxes were packed away, and the tree was pulled out of the corner and thrown roughly on the floor; then the servants dragged it out upon the staircase, where the daylight shone.

"Now life is beginning again," said the tree, rejoicing in the sunshine and fresh air. Then it was carried downstairs and taken into the courtyard so quickly that it forgot to think of itself and could only look about, there was so much to be seen.

The court was close to a garden, where everything looked blooming. Fresh and fragrant roses hung over the little palings. The linden trees were in blossom, while swallows flew here and there, crying, "Twit, twit, twit, my mate is coming"; but it was not the fir tree they meant.

"Now I shall live," cried the tree joyfully, spreading out its branches; but alas! they were all withered and yellow, and it lay in a corner among weeds and nettles. The star of gold paper still stuck in the top of the tree and glittered in the sunshine.

Two of the merry children who had danced round the tree at Christmas and had been so happy were playing in the same courtyard. The youngest saw the gilded star and ran and pulled it off the tree. "Look what is sticking to the ugly old fir tree," said the child, treading on the branches till they crackled under his boots.

And the tree saw all the fresh, bright flowers in the garden and then looked at itself and wished it had remained in the dark corner of the garret. It thought of its fresh youth in the forest, of the merry Christmas evening, and of the little mice who had listened to the story of Humpty Dumpty.

"Past! past!" said the poor tree. "Oh, had I but enjoyed myself while I could have done so! but now it is too late."

Then a lad came and chopped the tree into small pieces, till a large bundle lay in a heap on the ground. The pieces were placed in a fire, and they quickly blazed up brightly, while the tree sighed so deeply that each sigh was like a little pistol shot. Then the children who were at play came and seated themselves in front of the fire, and looked at it and cried, "Pop, pop." But at each "pop," which was a deep sigh, the tree was thinking of a summer day in the forest or of some winter night there when the stars shone brightly, and of Christmas evening, and of Humpty Dumpty—the only story it had ever heard or knew how to relate—till at last it was consumed.

The boys still played in the garden, and the youngest wore on his breast the golden star with which the tree had been adorned during the happiest evening of its existence. Now all was past; the tree's life was past and the story also past—for all stories must come to an end at some time or other.

# HARRIET BEECHER STOWE

## 1811-1896

# BETTY'S BRIGHT IDEA

*When He ascended up on high, He*
*led captivity captive, and gave gifts*
*unto men.*

*—Ephesians 4:8*

Some say that ever, 'gainst that season
    comes
Wherein our Saviour's birth is celebrate,
The bird of dawning singeth all night long.
And then, they say, no evil spirit walks;
The nights are wholesome; then no planets
    strike,

No fairy takes, no witch hath power to
    charm,—
So hallowed and so gracious is the time.

And this holy time, so hallowed and so gracious, was settling down over the great roaring, rattling, seething life-world of New York in the good year 1875. Who does not feel its on-coming in the shops and streets, in the festive air of trade and business, in the thousand garnitures by which every store hangs out triumphal banners and solicits you to buy something for a Christmas gift? For it is the peculiarity of all this array of prints, confectionery, dry goods, and manufactures of all kinds, that their bravery and splendor at Christmas tide is all to seduce you into generosity, and importune you to give something to others. It says to you, "The dear God gave you an unspeakable gift; give you a lesser gift to your brother!"

Do we ever think, when we walk those busy, bustling streets, all alive with Christmas shoppers, and mingle with the rushing tides that throng and jostle through the stores, that unseen spirits may be hastening to and fro along those same ways bearing Christ's Christmas gifts to men—gifts whose value no earthly gold or gems can represent?

Yet, on this morning of the day before Christmas, were these Shining Ones, moving to and fro with the crowd, whose faces were loving and serene as the invisible stars, whose robes took no defilement from the spatter and the rush of earth, whose coming and going was still as the falling snow-flakes. They entered houses without ringing door-bells, they passed through apartments without opening doors, and everywhere they were bearing Christ's Christmas presents, and silently offering them to whoever would open their souls to receive. Like themselves, their gifts were invisible—incapable of weight and measurement in gross earthly scales. To mourners they carried joy; to weary and perplexed hearts, peace; to souls stifling in luxury and self-indulgence they carried that noble discontent that rises to aspiration for higher things. Sometimes they took away an earthly treasure to make room for a heavenly one. They took health, but left resignation and cheerful faith. They took the babe from the dear cradle, but left in its place a heart full of pity for the suffering on earth and a fellowship with the blessed in heaven. Let us follow their footsteps awhile.

## Scene I

A young girl's boudoir in one of our American palaces of luxury, built after the choicest fancy of the architect, and furnished in all the latest devices of household decoration. Pictures, statuettes, and every form of *bijouterie* make the room a miracle of beauty, and the little princess of all sits in an easy chair before the fire, and thus revolves with herself:

"O, dear me! Christmas is a bore! Such a rush and crush in the streets, such a jam in the shops, and then *such* a fuss thinking up presents for everybody! All for nothing, too; for nobody wants anything. I'm sure *I* don't. I'm surfeited now with pictures and jewelry, and bon-bon boxes, and little china dogs and cats—and all these things that get so thick you can't move without upsetting some of them. There's papa, he don't want anything. He never uses any of my Christmas presents when I get them; and mamma, she has every earthly thing I can think of, and said the other day she did hope nobody'd give her any more worsted work! Then Aunt Maria and Uncle John, they don't want the things I give them; they have more than they know what to do with, now. All the boys say they don't want any more cigar cases or slippers, or smoking caps. Oh, dear!"

Here the Shining Ones came and stood over the little lady, and looked down on her with faces of pity, which seemed blent with a serene and half-amused indulgence. It was a heavenly amusement, such as that with which mothers listen to the foolish-wise prattle of children just learning to talk.

As the grave, sweet eyes rested tenderly on her, the girl somehow grew graver, leaned back in her chair, and sighed a little.

"I wish I knew how to be better!" she said to herself. "I remember last Sunday's text, 'It is more blessed to give than to receive.' That must mean something! Well, isn't there something, too, in the Bible about not giving to your rich neighbors that can give again, but giving to the poor that cannot recompense you? I don't know any poor people. Papa says there are very few deserving poor people. Well, for the matter of that, there aren't many *deserving rich* people. I, for example, how much do I *deserve* to have all these nice things? I'm no better than the poor shop-girls that go trudging by in the cold at six o'clock in the morning—ugh! it makes me shiver to think of it. I know if I had to do that *I* shouldn't be good at all. Well, I'd like to give to poor people, if I knew any."

At this moment the door opened and the maid entered.

"Betty, do you know any poor people I ought to get things for, this Christmas?"

"Poor folks is always plenty, miss," said Betty.

"O yes, of course, beggars; but I mean people that I could do something for besides just give cold victuals or money. I don't know where to hunt them up, and should be afraid to go if I did. O dear! It's no use. I'll give it up."

"Why, Miss Florence, that 'ud be too bad, afther bein' that good in yer heart, to let the poor folks alone for fear of goin' to them. But ye needn't do that, for, now I think of it, there's John Morley's wife."

"What, the gardener father turned off for drinking?"

"The same, miss. Poor boy, he's not so bad, and he's got a wife and two as pretty children as ever you see."

"I always liked John," said the young lady. "But papa is so strict about some things! He says he never will keep a man a day if he finds out that he drinks."

She was quite silent for a minute, and then broke out: "I don't care; it's a good idea! I say, Betty, do you know where John's wife lives?"

"Yes, miss, I've been there often."

"Well, then, this afternoon I'll go with you and see if I can do anything for them."


## Scene II


An attic room, neat and clean, but poorly furnished; a bed and a trundle-bed, a small cooking-stove, a shelf with a few dishes, one or two chairs and stools, a pale, thin woman working on a vest.

Her face is anxious; her thin hands tremble with weakness, and now and then, as she works, quiet tears drop, which she wipes quickly. Poor people cannot afford to shed tears; it takes time and injures eyesight.

This is John Morley's wife. This morning he has risen and gone out in a desperate mood. "No use to try," he says. "Didn't I go a whole year and never touch a drop? And now just because I fell once I'm kicked out! No use to try. When a fellow once trips, everybody gives him a kick. Talk about love of Christ! Who believes it? Don't see much love of Christ where I go. Your Christians hit a fellow that's down as hard as anybody. It's everybody for himself and devil take the hindmost. Well, I'll trudge up to the Brooklyn Navy Yard and see if they'll take me on there—if they won't I might as well go to sea, or to the devil," and out he flings.

"Mamma!" says a little voice, "what are we going to have for our Christmas?"

It is a little girl, with soft curly hair and bright, earnest eyes, that speaks.

A sturdy little fellow of four presses up to the

mother's knee and repeats the question, "Sha'n't we have a Christmas, mother?"

It overcomes the poor woman; she leans forward and breaks into sobbing—a tempest of sorrow, long suppressed, that shakes her weak frame as she thinks that her husband is out of work, desperate, discouraged, and tempted of the devil, that the rent is falling due, and only the poor pay of her needle to meet it with. In one of those quick flashes which concentrate through the imagination the sorrows of years, she seems to see her little home broken up, her husband in the gutter, her children turned into the street. At this moment there goes up from her heart a despairing cry, such as a poor, hunted, tired-out creature gives when brought to the last gasp of endurance. It was like the shriek of the hare when the hounds are upon it. She clasps her hands and cries out, "O my God, help me."

There was no voice of any that answered; there was no sound of foot-fall on the staircase; no one entered the door; and yet that agonized cry had reached the heart it was meant for. The Shining Ones were with her; they stood, with faces full of tenderness, beaming down upon her; they brought her a Christmas gift from Christ—the gift of trust. She knew not from whence came the courage and rest that entered her soul; but while her little ones stood wondering and silent, she turned and drew to herself her well-worn Bible. Hands that she did not see guided her as she turned the pages, and pointed the words: *He shall deliver the needy when he crieth; the poor also and him that hath no helper. He shall spare the poor and needy, and shall save the souls of the needy. He shall redeem their soul from deceit and violence, and precious shall their blood be in his sight.*

She laid down her poor wan cheek on the merciful old book, as on her mother's breast, and gave up all the tangled skein of life into the hands of Infinite Pity. There seemed a consoling presence in the room, and her tired heart found rest.

She wiped away her tears, kissed her children, and smiled upon them. Then she rose, gathered up her finished work, and attired herself to go forth and carry it back to the shop.

"Mother," said the children softly, "they are

dressing the church, and the gates are open, and people are going in and out; mayn't we play there by the church?"

The mother looked out on the ivy-grown walls of the church, with its flocks of twittering sparrows, and said: "Yes, my little birds; you may play there if you'll be very good and quiet."

The mother had only her small, close attic room for her darlings, and to satisfy all their childish desire for variety and motion, she had only the refuge of the streets. She was a decent, godly woman, and the bold manners and evil words of street vagrants were terrible to her; and so, when the church gates were open for daily morning and evening prayers, she had often begged the sexton to let her little ones come in and hear the singing, and wander hand in hand around the old church walls. He was a kindly old man, and the children, stealing round like two still, bright-eyed little mice, had gained upon his heart, and he made them welcome there. It gave the mother a feeling of protection to have them play near the church, as if it were a father's house.

So she put on their little hoods and tippets, and

led them forth, and saw them into the yard; and as she looked to the old gray church, with its rustling ivy bowers and flocks of birds, her heart swelled within her. "Yea, the sparrow hath found a house and the swallow a nest where she may lay her young, even thine altars, O Lord of hosts, my king and my God!" And the Shining Ones walking with her said, "Fear not; ye are of more value than many sparrows."

## Scene III

The little ones went gayly into the yard. They had been scared by their mother's tears; but she had smiled again, and that had made all right with them. The sun was shining brightly, and they were on the sunny side of the old church, and they laughed and chirped and chittered to each other as merrily as the little birds in the ivy boughs.

The old sexton came to the side door and threw out an armful of refuse greens, and then stopped a moment and nodded kindly at them.

"May we play with them, please, sir?" said the little Elsie, looking up with great reverence.

"Oh, yes, to be sure; these are done with—they are no good now."

"Oh, Tottie!" cried Elsie, rapturously, "just think, he says we may play with all these. Why, here's ever and ever so much green, enough to play house. Let's play build a house for father and mother."

"I'm going to build a big house for 'em when I grow up," said Tottie, "and I mean to have glass bead windows in it."

Tottie had once had presented to him a box of colored glass beads to string, and he could think of nothing finer in the future than unlimited glass beads.

Meanwhile, his sister began planting pine branches upright in the snow, to make her house.

"You see we can make believe there are windows and doors and a roof," she said, "and it's just as good. Now, let's make believe there is a bed in this corner, and we will lie down to sleep."

And Tottie obediently couched himself in the allotted corner and shut his eyes very hard, though after a moment he remarked that the snow got into his neck.

"You must play it isn't snow—play it's feathers," said Elsie.

"But I don't like it," persisted Tottie, "it don't feel a bit like feathers."

"Oh, well, then," said Elsie, accommodating herself to circumstances, "let's play get up now and I'll get breakfast."

Just now the door opened again, and the sexton began sweeping the refuse out of the church. There were bits of ivy and holly, and ruffles of ground-pine, and lots of bright red berries that came flying forth into the yard, and the children screamed for joy. "O Tottie!" "O Elsie!" "Only see how many pretty things—lots and lots!"

The sexton stood and looked and laughed as he saw the little ones so eager for the scraps and remnants.

"Don't you want to come in and see the church?" he said. "It's all done now, and a brave sight it is. You may come in."

They tipped in softly, with large bright, wondering

eyes. The light through the stained glass windows fell blue and crimson and yellow on the pillars all ruffled with ground-pine and brightened with scarlet bitter-sweet berries, and there were stars and crosses and mottoes in green all through the bowery aisles, while the organist, hid in a thicket of verdure, was practicing softly, and sweet voices sung:

"Hark! the herald angels sing

Glory to the new-born King."

The little ones wandered up and down the long aisles in a dream of awe and wonder. "Hush, Tottie!" said Elsie when he broke into an eager exclamation, "don't make a noise. I do believe it's something like heaven," she said, under her breath.

They made the course of the church and came round by the door again, where the sexton stood smiling on them.

"You can find lots of pretty Christmas greens out there," he said, pointing to the door; "perhaps your folks would like to have some."

"Oh, thank you, sir," exclaimed Elsie, rapturously. "Oh, Tottie, only think! Let's gather a good lot and go home and dress our room for Christmas.

Oh, *won't* mother be astonished when she comes home, we'll make it so pretty!"

And forthwith the children began gathering into their little aprons wreaths of ground-pine, sprigs of holly, and twigs of crimson bitter-sweet. The sexton, seeing their zeal, brought out to them a little cross, fancifully made of red alder-berries and pine.

Then he said, "A lady took that down to put up a bigger one, and she gave it to me; you may have it if you want it."

"Oh, how beautiful," said Elsie. "How glad I am to have this for mother! When she comes back she won't know our room; it will be as fine as the church."

Soon the little gleaners were toddling off out of the yard—moving masses of green with all that their aprons and their little hands could carry.

The sexton looked after them. "Take heed that ye despise not these little ones," he said to himself, "for in heaven their angels—"

A ray of tenderness fell on the old man's head; it was from the Shining One who watched the children. He thought it was an afternoon sunbeam. His heart grew gentle and peaceful, and his thoughts went far back to a distant green grove where his own little one was sleeping. "Seems to me I've loved all little ones ever since," he said, thinking far back to the Christmas week when his lamb was laid to rest. "Well, she shall not return to me, but I shall go to her." The smile of the Shining One made a warm glow in his heart, which followed him all the way home.

The children had a merry time dressing the room. They stuck good big bushes of pine in each window; they put a little ruffle of ground-pine round mother's Bible, and they fastened the beautiful red cross up over the table, and they stuck sprigs of pine or holly into every crack that could be made, by fair means or foul, to accept it, and they were immensely satisfied and delighted. Tottie insisted on hanging up his string of many-colored beads in the window to imitate the effect of the stained glass of the great church window.

"It looks pretty when the light comes through," he remarked; and Elsie admitted that they might play they were painted windows, with some show of propriety. When everything had been stuck somewhere, Elsie swept the floor, and made up a fire, and put on the tea-kettle, to have everything ready to strike mother favorably on her return.

## Scene IV

A freezing, bright, cold afternoon. "Cold as Christmas!" say cheery voices, as the crowds rush to and fro into shops and stores, and come out with hands full of presents.

"Yes, cold as Christmas," says John Morley. "I should think so! Cold enough for a fellow that can't get in anywhere—that nobody wants and nobody helps! I should think so."

John had been trudging all day from point to point, only to hear the old story: times were hard, work was dull, nobody wanted him, and he felt morose and surly—out of humor with himself and with everybody else.

It is true that his misfortunes were from his own fault; but that consideration never makes a man a particle more patient or good-natured—indeed, it is an additional bitterness in his cup. John was an

Englishman. When he first landed in New York from the old country, he had been wild and dissipated and given to drinking. But by his wife's earnest entreaties he had been persuaded to sign the temperance pledge, and had gone on prosperously keeping it for a year. He had a good place and good wages, and all went well with him till in an evil hour he met some of his former boon-companions, and was induced to have a social evening with them.

In the first half hour of that evening were lost the fruits of the whole year's self-denial and self-control. He was not only drunk that night, but he went off for a fortnight, and was drunk night after night, and came back to find that his master had discharged him in indignation. John thinks this over bitterly, as he thuds about in the cold and calls himself a fool.

Yet, if the truth must be confessed, John had not much "sense of sin," so called. He looked on himself as an unfortunate and rather ill-used man, for had he not tried very hard to be good, and gone a great while against the stream of evil inclination? and now, just for one yielding, he was pitched out of place, and everybody was turned against him! He thought this was hard measure. Didn't everybody hit wrong sometimes? Didn't rich fellows have their wine, and drink a little too much now and then? Yet nobody was down on *them*.

"It's only because I'm poor," said John. "Poor folks' sins are never pardoned. There's my good wife—poor girl!" and John's heart felt as if it were breaking, for he was an affectionate creature, and loved his wife and babies, and in his deepest consciousness he knew that he was the one at fault. We have heard much about the sufferings of the wives and children of men who are overtaken with drink; but what is not so well understood is the sufferings of the men themselves in their sober moments, when they feel that they are becoming a curse to all that are dearest to them. John's very soul was wrung within him to think of the misery he had brought on his wife and children—the greater miseries that might be in store for them. He was faint of heart; he was tired; he had eaten nothing for hours, and on ahead he saw a drinking saloon. Why shouldn't he go and take one good drink, and then pitch off a ferry-boat into the East River, and so end the whole miserable muddle of life altogether?

John's steps were turning that way, when one of the Shining Ones, who had watched him all day, came nearer and took his hand. He felt no touch; but at that moment there darted into his soul a thought of his mother, long dead, and he stopped irresolute, then turned to walk another way. The hand that was guiding him led him to turn a corner, and his curiosity was excited by a stream of people who seemed to be pressing into a building. A distant sound of singing was heard as he drew nearer, and soon he found himself passing with the multitude into a great prayer-meeting. The music grew more distinct as he went in. A man was singing in clear, penetrating tones:

"What means this eager, anxious throng,
　　Which moves with busy haste along;
　　These wondrous gatherings day by day;
　　What means this strange commotion, say?
　　In accents hushed the throng reply,
　　'Jesus of Nazareth passeth by!'"

John had but a vague idea of religion, yet something in the singing affected him; and, weary and

footsore and heartsore as he was, he sank into a seat
and listened with absorbed attention:

> "Jesus! 'tis he who once below
> Man's pathway trod in toil and woe;
> And burdened ones where'er he came
> Brought out their sick and deaf and lame.
> The blind rejoiced to hear the cry,
> 'Jesus of Nazareth passeth by!'
> "Ho, all ye heavy-laden, come!
> Here's pardon, comfort, rest, and home.
> Ye wanderers from a Father's face,
> Return, accept his proffered grace.
> Ye tempted ones, there's refuge nigh—
> 'Jesus of Nazareth passeth by!'"

A plain man, who spoke the language of plain
working-men, now arose and read from his Bible the
words which the angel of old spoke to the shepherds
of Bethlehem:

> "*Fear not, for behold, I bring you tidings
> of great joy, which shall be to all people, for*

*unto you is born this day a Saviour, which is Christ the Lord."*

The man went on to speak of this with an intense practical earnestness that soon made John feel as if *he*, individually, were being talked to; and the purport of the speech was this: that God had sent to him, John Morley, a Saviour to save him from his sins, to lift him above his weakness, to help him overcome his bad habits; that His name was called Jesus, because he shall save his people *from their sins*. John listened with a strange new thrill. This was what he needed—a Friend, all-powerful, all-pitiful, who would undertake for him and help him to overcome himself—for he sorely felt how weak he was. Here was a Friend that could have compassion on the ignorant and them that were out of the way. The thought brought tears to his eyes and a glow of hope to his heart. What if He *would* help him? for deep down in John's heart, worse than cold or hunger or weariness, was the dreadful conviction that he was a doomed man, that he should drink again as he had drunk, and never come to good, but fall lower and lower, and drag all who loved him down with him.

And was this mighty Saviour given to him?

"Yes," cried the man who was speaking; "to *you*; to you, who have lost name and place; to you, that nobody cares for; to you, who have been down in the gutter. God has sent you a Saviour to take you up out of the mud and mire, to wash you clean, to give you strength to overcome your sins, and lead you home to his blessed kingdom. This is the glad tidings of great joy that the angels brought on the first Christmas day. Christ was *God's Christmas gift* to a poor, lost world, and you may have him now, to-day. He may be your own Saviour—yours as much as if there were no other one on earth to be saved. He is looking for you to-day, coming after you, seeking you; he calls you by me. Oh, accept him now!"

There was a deep breathing of suppressed emotion as the speaker sat down, a pause of solemn stillness.

A faint strain of music was heard, and the singer

began singing a pathetic ballad of a lost sheep and
of the Shepherd going forth to seek it:

> "There were ninety and nine that safely lay
>     In the shelter of the fold,
> But one was out on the hills away,
>     Far off from the gates of gold—
> Away on the mountains wild and bare,
> Away from the tender Shepherd's care.
> "'Lord, Thou hast here Thy ninety and nine;
>     Are they not enough for Thee?'
> But the Shepherd made answer: 'Tis of mine
>     Has wandered away from me;
> And although the road be rough and steep
> I go to the desert to find my sheep.'"

John heard with an absorbed interest. All around
him were eager listeners, breathless, leaning forward
with intense attention. The song went on:

> "But none of the ransomed ever knew
>     How deep were the waters crossed;

Nor how dark was the night that
the Lord went through
Ere He found His sheep that was lost.
Out in the desert He heard its cry—
Sick and helpless, and ready to die."

There was a throbbing pathos in the intonation,
and the verse floated over the weeping throng; when,
after a pause, the strain was taken up triumphantly:

"But all through the mountains thunder-riven,
And up from the rocky steep,
There rose a cry to the gates of heaven,
'Rejoice! I have found my sheep!'
And the angels echoed around the throne,
'Rejoice, for the Lord brings back His own!'"

All day long, poor John had felt so lonesome!
Nobody cared for him; nobody wanted him; everything was against him; and, worst of all, he had no
faith in himself. But here was this Friend, *seeking* him,
following him through the cold alleys and crowded
streets. In heaven they would be glad to hear that he

had become a good man. The thought broke down all his pride, all his bitterness; he wept like a little child; and the Christmas gift of Christ—the sense of a real, present, loving, pitying Saviour—came into his very *soul*.

He went homeward as one in a dream. He passed the drinking-saloon without a thought or wish of drinking. The expulsive force of a new emotion had for the time driven out all temptation. Raised above weakness, he thought only of this Jesus, this Saviour from sin, who he now believed had followed him and found him, and he longed to go home and tell his wife what great things the Lord had done for him.

## Scene V

Meanwhile a little drama had been acting in John's humble home. His wife had been to the shop that day and come home with the pittance for her work in her hands.

"I'll pay you full price to-day, but we can't pay

such prices any longer," the man had said over the counter as he paid her. "Hard times—work dull—we are cutting down all our work-folks; you'll have to take a third less next time."

"I'll do my best," she said meekly, as she took her bundle of work and turned wearily away, but the invisible arm of the Shining One was round her, and the words again thrilled through her that she had read that morning: "He shall redeem their soul from deceit and violence, and precious shall their blood be in his sight." She saw no earthly helper; she heard none and felt none, and yet her soul was sustained, and she came home in peace.

When she opened the door of her little room she drew back astonished at the sight that presented itself. A brisk fire was roaring in the stove, and the tea-kettle was sputtering and sending out clouds of steam. A table with a white cloth on it was drawn out before the fire, and a new tea set of pure white cups and saucers, with teapot, sugar-bowl, and creamer, complete, gave a festive air to the whole. There were bread, and butter, and ham-sandwiches, and a Christmas cake all frosted, with little blue and red and green candles round it ready to be lighted, and a bunch of hot-house flowers in a pretty little vase in the centre.

A new stuffed rocking-chair stood on one side of the stove, and there sat Miss Florence De Witt, our young princess of Scene First, holding little Elsie in her lap, while the broad, honest countenance of Betty was beaming with kindness down on the delighted face of Tottie. Both children were dressed from head to foot in complete new suits of clothes, and Elsie was holding with tender devotion a fine doll, while Tottie rejoiced in a horse and cart which he was maneuvering under Betty's superintendence.

The little princess had pleased herself in getting up all this tableau. Doing good was a novelty to her, and she plunged into it with the zest of a new amusement. The amazed look of the poor woman, her dazed expressions of rapture and incredulous joy, the shrieks and cries of confused delight with which the little ones met their mother, delighted her more than any scene she had ever witnessed at the opera—with this added grace, unknown to her, that at this scene the invisible Shining Ones were pleased witnesses.

She had been out with Betty, buying here and there whatever was wanted—and what was *not* wanted for those who had been living so long without work or money?

She had their little coal-bin filled, and a nice pile of wood and kindlings put behind the stove. She had bought a nice rocking-chair for the mother to rest in. She had dressed the children from head to foot at a ready-made clothing store, and bought them toys to their hearts' desire, while Betty had set the table for a Christmas feast.

And now she said to the poor woman at last:

"I'm so sorry John lost his place at father's. He was so kind and obliging, and I always liked him; and I've been thinking, if you'd get him to sign the pledge over again from Christmas Eve, never to touch another drop, I'll get papa to take him back. I always do get papa to do what I want, and the fact is, he hasn't got anybody that suited him so well since John left. So you tell John that I mean to go surety for him; he certainly won't fail *me*. Tell him *I trust him.*" And Miss Florence pulled out a paper wherein, in her best round hand, she had written out again the temperance pledge, and dated it *"Christmas Eve, 1875."*

"Now, you come with John to-morrow morning, and bring this with his name to it, and you'll see what I'll do!" and, with a kiss to the children, the little good fairy departed, leaving the family to their Christmas Eve.

What that Christmas Eve was, when the husband and father came home with the new and softened heart that had been given him, who can say? There were joyful tears and solemn prayers, and earnest vows and purposes of a new life heard by the Shining Ones in the room that night.

"And the angels echoed around the throne,
Rejoice! for the Lord brings back his own."

## Scene VI

"Now, papa, I want you to give me something special to-day, because it's Christmas," said the little princess to her father, as she kissed and wished him "Merry Christmas" next morning.

267

"What is it, Pussy—half of my kingdom?"

"No, no, papa; not so much as that. It's a little bit of my own way that I want."

"Of course; well, what is it?"

"Well, I want you to take John back again."

Her father's face grew hard.

"Now, please, papa, don't say a word till you have heard me. John was a capital gardener; he kept the green-house looking beautiful; and this Mike that we've got now, he's nothing but an apprentice, and stupid as an owl at that! He'll never do in the world."

"All that is very true," said Mr. De Witt, "but *John drinks*, and I *won't* have a drinking man."

"But, papa, *I* mean to take care of that. I've written out the temperance pledge, and dated it, and got John to sign it, and *here it is*," and she handed the paper to her father, who read it carefully, and sat turning it in his hands while his daughter went on:

"You ought to have seen how poor, how very poor they were. His wife is such a nice, quiet, hard-working woman, and has two such pretty children. I went to see them and carry them Christmas things yesterday, but it's no good doing anything if John can't get work. She told me how the poor fellow had been walking the streets in the cold, day after day, trying everywhere, and nobody would take him. It's a dreadful time now for a man to be out of work, and it isn't fair his poor wife and children should suffer. Do try him again, papa!"

"John always did better with the pineapples than anybody we have tried," said Mrs. De Witt at this point. "He is the only one who really understands pineapples."

At this moment the door opened, and there was a sound of chirping voices in the hall. "Please, Miss Florence," said Betty, "the little folks says they wants to give you a Christmas." She added in a whisper: "They thinks much of giving you something, poor little things—plaze take it of 'em." And little Tottie at the word marched in and offered the young princess his dear, beautiful, beloved string of glass beads, and Elsie presented the cross of red berries— most dear to her heart and fair to her eyes. "We wanted to give *you something*," she said bashfully.

"Oh, you lovely dears!" cried Florence; "how sweet of you! I shall keep these beautiful glass beads always, and put the cross up over my dressing-table. I thank you *ever* so much!"

"Are those John's children?" asked Mr. De Witt, winking a tear out of his eye—he was at bottom a soft-hearted old gentleman.

"Yes, papa," said Florence, caressing Elsie's curly hair, "see how sweet they are!"

"Well—you may tell John I'll try him again." And so passed Florence's Christmas, with a new, warm sense of joy in her heart, a feeling of something in the world to be done, worth doing.

"How much joy one can give with a little money!" she said to herself as she counted over what she had spent on her Christmas. Ah yes! and how true that "It *is* more blessed to give than to receive." A shining, invisible hand was laid on her head in blessing as she lay down that night, and a sweet sense of a loving presence stole like music into her soul. Unknown to herself, she had that day taken the first step out of self-life into that life of love and care for others which brought the King of Glory down to share earth's toils and sorrows. And that precious experience was Christ's Christmas gift to her.

POEMS

CLEMENT CLARKE MOORE

1779–1863

# A VISIT FROM ST. NICHOLAS

*(or, 'Twas the Night Before Christmas)*

'Twas the night before Christmas, when all through
    the house
Not a creature was stirring, not even a mouse;
The stockings were hung by the chimney
    with care,
In hopes that St. Nicholas soon would be there;
The children were nestled all snug in their beds,
While visions of sugar-plums danced in their heads;
And mamma in her 'kerchief, and I in my cap,
Had just settled our brains for a long winter's nap,
When out on the lawn there arose such a clatter,
I sprang from the bed to see what was the matter.

Away to the window I flew like a flash,
Tore open the shutters and threw up the sash.
The moon on the breast of the new-fallen snow
Gave the lustre of mid-day to objects below,
When, what to my wondering eyes should appear,
But a miniature sleigh, and eight tiny reindeer,
With a little old driver, so lively and quick,
I knew in a moment it must be St. Nick.
More rapid than eagles his coursers they came,
And he whistled, and shouted, and called them
    by name;
"Now, *Dasher*! now, *Dancer*! now, *Prancer* and
    *Vixen*!
On, *Comet*! on, *Cupid*! on, *Donner* and *Blitzen*!
To the top of the porch! to the top of the wall!
Now dash away! dash away! dash away all!"
As dry leaves that before the wild hurricane fly,
When they meet with an obstacle, mount to the sky;
So up to the house-top the coursers they flew,
With the sleigh full of Toys, and St. Nicholas too.
And then, in a twinkling, I heard on the roof
The prancing and pawing of each little hoof.
As I drew in my head, and was turning around,

Down the chimney St. Nicholas came with a
    bound.
He was dressed all in fur, from his head to his foot,
And his clothes were all tarnished with ashes
    and soot;
A bundle of Toys he had flung on his back,
And he looked like a peddler just opening
    his pack.
His eyes—how they twinkled! his dimples how
    merry!
His cheeks were like roses, his nose like a cherry!
His droll little mouth was drawn up like a bow
And the beard of his chin was as white as the snow;
The stump of a pipe he held tight in his teeth,
And the smoke it encircled his head like a wreath;
He had a broad face and a little round belly,
That shook when he laughed, like a bowlful of jelly.
He was chubby and plump, a right jolly old elf,
And I laughed when I saw him, in spite of myself;
A wink of his eye and a twist of his head,
Soon gave me to know I had nothing to dread;
He spoke not a word, but went straight to his work,
And filled all the stockings; then turned with a jerk,

And laying his finger aside of his nose,
And giving a nod, up the chimney he rose;
He sprang to his sleigh, to his team gave a whistle,
And away they all flew like the down of a thistle,
But I heard him exclaim, ere he drove out of sight,
*"Happy Christmas to all, and to all a good-night."*

# ELIZABETH BARRETT BROWNING

1806-1861

# THE HOLY NIGHT

We sate among the stalls at Bethlehem;
The dumb kine from their fodder turning them,
Softened their horn'd faces,
To almost human gazes
Toward the newly Born:
The simple shepherds from the star-lit brooks
Brought visionary looks,
As yet in their astonished hearing rung
The strange sweet angel-tongue:
The magi of the East, in sandals worn,
Knelt reverent, sweeping round,
With long pale beards, their gifts upon the ground,

The incense, myrrh, and gold
These baby hands were impotent to hold:
So let all earthlies and celestials wait
Upon thy royal state.
Sleep, sleep, my kingly One!

# HENRY WADSWORTH LONGFELLOW

1807-1882

# THE THREE KINGS

Three Kings came riding from far away,
Melchior and Gaspar and Baltasar;
Three Wise Men out of the East were they,
And they travelled by night and they slept by day,
For their guide was a beautiful, wonderful star.

The star was so beautiful, large and clear,
That all the other stars of the sky
Became a white mist in the atmosphere,
And by this they knew that the coming was near
Of the Prince foretold in the prophecy.

Three caskets they bore on their saddle-bows,
Three caskets of gold with golden keys;

Their robes were of crimson silk with rows
Of bells and pomegranates and furbelows,
Their turbans like blossoming almond-trees.

And so the Three Kings rode into the West,
Through the dusk of the night, over hill and dell,
And sometimes they nodded with beard on
    breast,
And sometimes talked, as they paused to rest,
With the people they met at some wayside well.

"Of the child that is born," said Baltasar,
"Good people, I pray you, tell us the news;
For we in the East have seen his star,
And have ridden fast, and have ridden far,
To find and worship the King of the Jews."

And the people answered, "You ask in vain;
We know of no King but Herod the Great!"
They thought the Wise Men were men insane,
As they spurred their horses across the plain,
Like riders in haste, who cannot wait.

And when they came to Jerusalem,
Herod the Great, who had heard this thing,
Sent for the Wise Men and questioned them;
And said, "Go down unto Bethlehem,
And bring me tidings of this new king."

So they rode away; and the star stood still,
The only one in the grey of morn;
Yes, it stopped—it stood still of its own free will,
Right over Bethlehem on the hill,
The city of David, where Christ was born.

And the Three Kings rode through the gate and
    the guard,
Through the silent street, till their horses turned
And neighed as they entered the great inn-yard;
But the windows were closed, and the doors were
    barred,
And only a light in the stable burned.

And cradled there in the scented hay,
In the air made sweet by the breath of kine,

The little child in the manger lay,
The child, that would be king one day
Of a kingdom not human, but divine.

His mother Mary of Nazareth
Sat watching beside his place of rest,
Watching the even flow of his breath,
For the joy of life and the terror of death
Were mingled together in her breast.

They laid their offerings at his feet:
The gold was their tribute to a King,
The frankincense, with its odor sweet,
Was for the Priest, the Paraclete,
The myrrh for the body's burying.

And the mother wondered and bowed her head,
And sat as still as a statue of stone,
Her heart was troubled yet comforted,
Remembering what the Angel had said
Of an endless reign and of David's throne.

Then the Kings rode out of the city gate,
With a clatter of hoofs in proud array;
But they went not back to Herod the Great,
For they knew his malice and feared his hate,
And returned to their homes by another way.

# PAUL LAURENCE DUNBAR

1872-1906

# CHRISTMAS CAROL

Ring out, ye bells!
    All Nature swells
With gladness at the wondrous story,—
    The world was lorn,
    But Christ is born
To change our sadness into glory.

    Sing, earthlings, sing!
    To-night a King
Hath come from heaven's high throne to
    bless us.
    The outstretched hand
    O'er all the land
Is raised in pity to caress us.

Come at his call;
Be joyful all;
Away with mourning and with sadness!
The heavenly choir
With holy fire
Their voices raise in songs of gladness.

The darkness breaks
And Dawn awakes,
Her cheeks suffused with youthful blushes.
The rocks and stones
In holy tones
Are singing sweeter than the thrushes.

Then why should we
In silence be,
When Nature lends her voice to praises;
When heaven and earth
Proclaim the truth
Of Him for whom that lone star blazes?

No, be not still,
But with a will
Strike all your harps and set them ringing;
On hill and heath
Let every breath
Throw all its power into singing!

# CHRISTINA ROSSETTI

1830-1894

# CHRISTMAS EVE

Christmas hath a darkness
    Brighter than the blazing noon,
Christmas hath a chillness
    Warmer than the heat of June,
Christmas hath a beauty
    Lovelier than the world can show:
For Christmas bringeth Jesus,
    Brought for us so low.

Earth, strike up your music,
    Birds that sing and bells that ring;
Heaven hath answering music
    For all Angels soon to sing:

Earth, put on your whitest
    Bridal robe of spotless snow:
For Christmas bringeth Jesus,
    Brought for us so low.

# MARGARET DELAND

1857-1945

# THE WAITS

At the break of Christmas Day,
   Through the frosty starlight ringing,
Faint and sweet and far away,
   Comes the sound of children, singing,
      Chanting, singing,
      "*Cease to mourn,*
      *For Christ is born,*
         *Peace and joy to all men bringing!*"

Careless that the chill winds blow,
   Growing stronger, sweeter, clearer,

Noiseless footfalls in the snow,
    Bring the happy voices nearer;
        Hear them singing,
     *"Winter's drear,*
    *But Christ is here,*
        *Mirth and gladness with Him*
*bringing."*

"Merry Christmas!" hear them say,
    As the East is growing lighter;
"May the joy of Christmas Day
    Make your whole year gladder, brighter!"
        Join their singing,
     *"To each home*
    *Our Christ has come,*
        *All Love's treasures with Him*
*bringing!"*

# LIBBIE C. BAER

1849-1929

# WHEN CHRISTMAS COMES

(Harry.)

When Christmas comes my brother Fred
And I are each to have a sled,
So papa says. To all *good* boys
Old Santa brings both books and toys,
    When Christmas comes.

(Paul.)

I know my mother is too poor,
To buy us toys, but I am sure
She'll have for us some nice warm caps,
Some mittens, and some shoes, perhaps,
    When Christmas comes.

(James.)

I wrote old Santa Claus to bring
To me a drum, and everything;
A train of cars to run by steam,
And all of which I think, and dream,
When Christmas comes.

(Willie.)

You greedy boy! You want it all;
I only want a top and ball;
I want what Santa Claus can spare
When *other* boys have had their share,
When Christmas comes.

(James.)

I only wrote old Santa Claus
To bring me all those things, because
I want to *give away* some toys,
To *Paul*, and other widows' boys,
When Christmas comes.

(John.)

That's right, my chum,
With fife and drum,
And singing tops we'll make things hum;
Divide our toys with other boys,
And won't we make a sight of noise,
When Christmas comes.

(All.)

When Christmas comes to you and me,
Bid every selfish thought to flee;
Unselfish hearts and deeds, and then,
"Peace on earth, good will to men,"
When Christmas comes.

ANNA DE BRÉMONT

1864–1922

# CHRISTMAS MORN

There's a holy light like a beacon bright,
      Afar over land and sea.
Soft its lambent ray o'er the broad earth plays
      With a rosy dancing glee,
And the topmost peak of the mountains bleak
      Blush fair in the glowing morn.
Over wood and tarn sweeps the glorious dawn
      To herald the Child-Christ born.

White the sea-waves fling like an angel's wing
      The foam as their blue crests rise,
While each gallant ship, with a skim and a dip,
      In the wind's lap speeding flies;

And the sailor's song is borne along
      The breeze of the golden morn,
For joyous he sings as the mast he swings
      To herald the Child-Christ born.

In the land of snow where the keen winds blow
      And the ice-king holds his sway,
A glittering sheen on the plains is seen,
      As tribute to him they pay.
While merrily sing with a peal and a ring
      The bells on the crystal morn,
As gayly they chime with silvery rhyme
      To herald the Child-Christ born.

To his sea-girt home, where'er he may roam,
      Speed the thoughts of Briton's son.
In city or plain, on the crested main,
      The heart of the absent one
Again in his dreams with ecstasy seems
      To swell in the happy morn,
As he hears the voice of his loved rejoice,
      To herald the Child-Christ born.

In dreams borne along, he joins the glad throng,
  The riot and wassail gay;
And the boar's head bold as in Nowel old
  Brave crowns the feast of the day;
The holly's red blush 'mid the ivy's crush;
  The mistletoe greets the morn
With kisses to claim in love's holy name,
  To herald the Child-Christ born.

Then Charity sweet with most gracious feet
  Walks forth o'er the smiling land,
To widow's relief, to fatherless grief,
  She bringeth a helping hand.
For peace and good-will the whole world doth fill
  With the dawn of the Nowel morn.
Let every heart sing a glad welcoming,
  To herald the Child-Christ born.